COLT CROSSING

Morgan was halfway to the faint lights of the saloons on Main Street when he saw shadows beside him. Two of them. He stabbed for his six-gun as a shot blasted almost in his face. He felt one of them kick his holster and his hand, sending the weapon out of leather and into the dust. There was no time to find the Colt because the two were on him, knives flashing in the pale moonlight.

One hand grabbed his shoulder and spun him around. They hesitated a moment, knives ready, a pair of experienced men who knew how to kill a man quickly and silently. Morgan figured they probably enjoyed their work....

Also in the *Buckskin* Series:

BUCKSKIN #24

COLT CROSSING

KIT DALTON

LEISURE BOOKS NEW YORK CITY

A LEISURE BOOK®

March 2005

Published by

Dorchester Publishing Co., Inc.
200 Madison Avenue
New York, NY 10016

ISBN 0-8439-2728-3

Printed in the United States of America.

Visit us on the web at www.dorchesterpub.com.

COLT
CROSSING

Chapter One

"What do you mean, I pushed you?" the smaller of the two men standing next to the bar and glaring at each other said softly. He was barely over five feet tall, wearing a black suit, a white shirt and string tie.

The fancy red and black vest and the half contained manner of a man who always controlled his outward show of emotions screamed "gambler" for any who chose to guess. He was clean shaven, about thirty five and had the look of a man who had put up with a lot of outrageous situations in his time.

"You little fart! You pushed my shoulder and made me slosh my beer all over my sleeve. You buy me a new beer or I'll ram this glass down your throat!" The taller man was a shade under six feet. He had grown heavy in his mid years and a roll of fat edged over his gunbelt and sagged his jowls.

He had a two-day's growth of beard and some-where he'd lost his hat. More than enough whiskey and beer had turned him into an angry, violent drunk.

The gambler shook his head and tossed a dime on the counter. "Two beers for the town drunk here," the small man said. He turned and stared into the taller man's eyes. "You got two beers to soak up, now leave me alone. Besides, I didn't push your damned shoulder!"

The big man dropped his beer mug on the bar. It shattered, splashing the half glass of brew in every direction. He didn't notice the crash. His big hand fisted and drove into the gambler's face, mashing his nose, breaking off two teeth and blasting him four feet down the side of the bar.

Lee Morgan lifted his beer off the middle of the bar and moved back out of the combat zone. Just another barroom brawl. He'd seen a dozen since he'd arrived here two hours earlier.

The gambler spit out another tooth, his face flooded with anger and he stormed at the taller man, his fists measured and sure, jabbing repeatedly at the attacker's face in a classic display of fine boxing. The punches stung and drew blood from the tall man's nose, then the corner of his mouth.

"Little bastard!" the taller one screeched. His fists blasted out like pile drivers as they swung with more force than skill. Most missed the bobbing and weaving target, but one hit the gambler in the chest, jolting him back a step. The gambler's rage grew as he darted in again, landing three quick jabs which brought a spout of blood from the tall man's nose.

"Little shithead!" the bleeding man roared. He charged forward this time, absorbing two jabs to his face, then grabbed the gambler and squeezed him in a bear hug that took the fight out of him. The gambler struggled to catch his breath.

Then the big man picked the gambler up shoulder high and smashed him down onto a poker table where two players scrambled to get free.

The gambler hit and broke the table, rolled to the floor and eased up to his feet. His left hand drew a derringer from his inside vest pocket and he swung it up as his attacker came forward again. The little gun fired with a surprisingly loud report as the slug sliced through an inch of the tall man's arm. The drunk charged forward, evidently not even noticing the wound, and swatted the derringer out of the gambler's hand. The small gun clattered to the floor eliminating the second round.

The big man stared at the gambler for a moment, roared in pain and fury, then he picked up the smaller man and held him over his head. He grunted and slammed the gambler against the top of the bar. His body struck the sturdy wooden bar with the middle of his back. It made a crack that everyone in the saloon heard.

The gambler's body hung there a moment, his head and shoulders across the top of the bar, his torso and legs hanging at an unnatural angle down the front of the bar.

"My god, broke his back!" somebody said in the hush.

Then the body, once owned by the gambler, slid down the front of the bar into the sawdust on the floor.

"Is he dead?" someone asked.

"If he ain't I bet he wishes he was," a voice answered.

The tall man who had thrown the gambler stood panting, his eyes still wide, his face flushed with anger. Large hands hung at the ends of his arms twitching now and then. Around his waist was a six-gun tied low on a cartridge belt.

The barkeep came around the end of the bar which had been built on top of a pair of barrels and viewed the remains. He bent and looked into the gambler's eyes, then squatted and put his ear to the white shirt now splattered with the attacker's blood. The apron stood and shook his head.

"Reckon somebody better go for the sheriff," the bar man said. A man volunteered and ran out the door.

Lee Morgan eased into a chair at a poker table and scowled as he stared at the big killer and the dead man crumbled in the sawdust of the "barrel-house" cheap saloon.

What a wonderful way to be introduced to a new town. He'd been here less than two hours and already he'd seen a man killed by a brutal, drunken fool. Morgan eyed the killer's six-gun, saw the way it hung low and the bottom of the leather holster tied down tight against his thigh so there would be no movement of leather when the man slapped for iron.

No, the man was not a lout, he was a gunfighter, who got so drunk he forgot his gun and went to his more basic instincts. That was a quick way for a fast gunman to wake up and find out that he was dead.

Morgan watched the men, about twenty of them in this oversized tent that bragged that it was the best saloon in town. Half of the stores on Main Street were still tents here in North Platte in the brand new state of Nebraska.

It was 281 miles due west of Omaha on the equally new Union Pacific railroad. A year ago it had been nothing but a tent city, a railroad construction town. It was the kind that flourished every ten miles or so along the right of way and attracted the lowest available gamblers, cutthroats, prostitutes, con-men and killers in the surrounding hundred miles.

There was money to be made in a railroad construction tent city. They attracted the worst of every vice like flies to fresh horse droppings.

By now the "Hell on Wheels" reputation of this small rail town had been somewhat moderated. The hell was still here, but the "wheels" of the railroad construction workers had moved on down the line in the race toward Utah and the eventual hoped-for-completion of the Transcontinental Railroad. The dream would some day be a reality.

Every fifty miles the railroad builders were supposed to establish permanent towns. Morgan had no idea if this was one of the permanent ones, or if the small trading post that had been established here at the confluence of the South Platte and the North Platte rivers had lasted this long by pure chance.

The sheriff of Lincoln County, Emery Lewis, hurried in the door, swore softly. The lawman was five-feet five-inches tall with a growing pot belly, a leather vest with a sheriff's star pinned on it and a well worn, brown, low crowned hat with the brims curved up. His face was lined and weathered.

Now he stared at the tall man. "Wild Bill, you drunk again? Sonsbitch! What am I gonna do with you? You kill this poor fellah?"

The man called Wild Bill had a glaze over his eyes as he stared at the sheriff.

"What?"

"Wild Bill Nelson!" the sheriff said with more force. "Did you kill this man?"

"Hell, sheriff, it was a fair fight," a drinker at

the bar said.

"That so?"

"Sure enough," a young cowboy spoke up. "Gambler man there pulled his derringer out and shot old Wild Bill in the arm. Made him right mad and more than a little bit concerned about the second round and the state of his general health."

There was laughter. The sheriff looked at the barkeep.

"Vern, how'd you see it?"

"Mostly busy, but I seen the gambler there get into a pushing game with Wild Bill and then somebody got slugged and it got out of hand. Yeah, the gambler shot Wild Bill."

Sheriff Lewis stood there a minute with hands on his hips. He carried a gun but didn't look like he used it much. At last he nodded. "All right, good enough for me. Self defense. Two of you get this body over to the undertaker. If there's nobody there, leave him by the back door. He won't walk off nowhere." A few men guffawed at the remark. "First let me get his identification and his valuables. Where's the derringer?"

A man at a poker table held it out to the Sheriff.

"Oh, anybody know the gambler's name?" the lawman asked.

"Yeah, I played a couple of hands with him," a man at a poker table volunteered. "Told me his name was Ben Allison, but can't swear he was truth saying."

"It'll do," the Sheriff said and walked out behind the men carrying the body.

Lee Morgan put his mug of beer down quickly when he heard the dead man's name. So far this assignment was one problem after another one. Ben Allison had been one of the few leads he had in this town. He was supposed to talk to Allison as soon as he could find the man. Now that one sure contact was just plain shot all to hell.

Morgan left the rest of his beer and went out to the street. North Platte stood in the middle of the great plains, with the horizon meeting the flatness of the farm and ranch land in a 360-degree circle. Everywhere you looked, flat land lay ready for the plow or the hooves of beef cattle and the branding iron.

The town had done well for being less than two years old. Morgan heard this little town even had a newspaper, the *Pioneer on Wheels*. The name came from the fact that the paper was published from a box car sitting on a siding. If this little town folded, he could just hook up to the next train and move to the next town down the line. Maybe the press was too heavy to unload from the rail car.

More than twenty frame buildings showed down the main street. No street names were in evidence. The tent structures were mostly framed up with the tents spread over them. They were the real leftovers from the construction site businesses.

Whores still walked the streets. They were by far the majority of females in town so they went where they pleased and did as they pleased. Many of them carried small revolvers and derringers openly.

Morgan watched a pair of soiled doves walking past him in the early afternoon sunshine. They were painted, brazen, enticing in a crude sort of way. Morgan waved them on past and watched their bottoms twitching down the boardwalk. He had heard that no whore had been tried or even charged in the dozens of killings that they dealt out in these railroad construction towns. Things would quiet down here eventually.

But not before he had a hand in stirring them up a little. He leaned against the hardware store and snorted. His first and best contact dead. So he went to the next one on his long list of two. For a minute he wished he had never taken this job back in Omaha.

Chapter Two

Lee Morgan had received the telegram at the fancy New West Hotel in Denver. It was an interesting offer. Ten thousand dollars was a fortune to most men. Morgan had made and lost that much once or twice, but right now he was what he liked to refer to as a mite bit short. Along with the telegram was authorization to ride on a pass on the Union Pacific from wherever he was to Omaha.

Most of the West was undergoing what folks called "hard times." A cowboy worked 18 hours a day for $25 and found a month's work on the good spreads. A clerk might take home $28 to $30 a month. Beer was a nickel a mug full, and whiskey ten cents a shot. A fresh loaf of bread at the bakery cost seven cents and you could stay at a good hotel in the West for fifty cents a night, bathwater extra.

Ten thousand dollars was a working man's pay for almost 28 years. Now that's a powerful lot of cash money to any man, and Lee Morgan had been without gainful employment for over a month. What the hell, he was getting a free train ride to Omaha.

But it was *railroad money!*

In the west along about that time, before the transcontinental rail link had been completed, the railroad was Savior or Satan, depending on who you were and whether the long steel tracks and the huffing and puffing locomotives made or ruined your fortunes and your personal livelihood.

Lee Morgan was a gun for hire, and usually he wasn't all that particular about who it was he carried the iron for. He shied away from downright fraud and the thievery jobs, but he was not known to turn down a dollar or two because it might have some taint on it concerning the legality of the transaction.

Morgan kicked off the coach rail car in Omaha. He'd ridden the steam engine pulled cars before. Sure as hell beat riding your ass off on a horse to move your body six or seven hundred miles. Best part of rail travel was that it was so fast: thirty-five miles an hour, day and night—over six hundred miles on a good 24-hour day if the tracks weren't washed out by a cloudburst or there weren't a thousand buffalo munching their unhurried way across the tracks.

Three men standing in front of rigs drawn up in front of the fancy station waved at him.

"Take you wherever you need to go for a quarter," one man called.

The next offered to do the job for fifteen cents. By the time Morgan had walked up with his well worn carpetbag, they all offered him their hacks for a dime.

He picked the youngest and tossed him the dime.

"Yes, sir! Where you going, mister?"

Morgan gave him the address and the boy, not much over sixteen laughed. "I could drive you around a few blocks and then take you there," the youth admitted. "But it's right across the street, the Union Pacific Railroad General Headquarters Building."

He tossed the dime back to Morgan. Lee caught the coin, stepped in the rig, then handed the ten cents back to the youth.

"Drive me," Morgan said.

Twenty minutes later, Morgan tipped a glass filled with whiskey, branch water and chunks of ice and drank slowly. It was good Tennessee sippin' whiskey. Why did they want to spoil it with water?

Morgan waited for about twenty minutes. The same man who had greeted him and fixed the drink for him checked with him again and said Mr. Johnson would be with him in a few moments. The office Morgan was in was twenty feet square, with elk and moose heads on the paneled wall. A model of a railroad train sat on a table complete with stations, switches and little cars that rolled along the tracks. The whole place was expensively furnished, and had the feeling of power and authority.

A half hour later, three men came into the room. One was shorter than the other two, but he clearly was in command.

"Then pay what they ask, but remind them the next time we do business with them it will be at our price." The man was solid, square cut as a block of granite and looked just as hard. He was no more than 55, his hair black and full, dark eyebrows over strangely light blue eyes, and a large nose that had been broken and never quite healed straight.

The man looked up and saw Morgan standing by

the cold fireplace near the collection of decorative whiskey bottles.

"Ah, Mr. Morgan. Lew told me you were here." He marched across the twenty foot wide office and held out his hand. "I'm Quenton Johnson, your new boss—if you've decided to come to work with us."

Morgan gripped the surprisingly strong hand and nodded. "Afternoon, Mr. Johnson. The pay is adequate, but I'll need to know more about the job. I don't buy in on a blind hand."

"Indeed you shouldn't, but don't think you can raise the pot, it's set. The work is simple. You're aware of the land grants the railroads receive for completing each mile of track as we blast across the plains toward the General Pacific's end of the line."

"Yes."

"Good. The process of selecting, checking, authorizing, and then double checking these land grant papers is all highly complicated and takes a lot of time. That's my problem, not yours.

"When it is all finished, the paper we get is called a land patent deed. Without that patent, the land is worthless to us because we can't sell it, lease it, or do anything with it. Is that clear?"

"I've owned land, Mr. Johnson. It's something like a grant deed?"

"Yes. When the government sells land they call it a patent deed, and everyone else says it's a grant deed. Same thing. These are handled by a number of different governmental agencies and when the last step is taken, the General Land Office in Washington D.C. grants the patent deeds and forwards them to the railroad. For some bureaucratic reason, the patents have to be sent to the firm in the land office district in which they were first filed."

"Your problem is that you're missing some of

those patents and want me to find them for you. Is that right?"

Johnson took a step back, nodded. "Yes, yes, exactly right. 'Some' is an understatement. We get the land in grants for twenty miles at a time. Right now we get twenty sections of land for every mile of track we lay. For twenty miles of track that's four hundred sections of land, or two hundred and fifty-six thousand acres. We're missing two of those land grant packets of patents, for over a half million acres of land."

Morgan whistled. "Now that is a big chunk of land to have missing."

The two men who had come into the room with Johnson had worked to the sides of the room and now stood without moving. Morgan could tell both men were armed with concealed weapons. His own tied low .45 remained in place on his thigh.

Morgan sipped his drink, then walked to the big window and looked out. "How cold is the trail?"

"It's been over six months since the patents were sent from Washington by special courier. A special man always brings them in a satchel looked by a chain to his left wrist. The patents are not negotiable like paper currency, or bearer bonds. They are no good to anyone else without the proper company signatures on them. Still, someone stole them."

"You had Pinkerton on the job?"

"Yes, how did you know?" Johnson asked, turning toward him with surprise.

"They are the best detectives in the country. For this job you need a detective. That's not what I am. I'm a hired gun. I do jobs that need doing where my gun, and the way I use it, play an important part."

"Yes, we engaged the Pinkertons on this case, but they made no headway, learned nothing in four months, so we discharged them. I asked around for the best man in the West for this difficult job. Three people I trust mentioned your name, but each said you wouldn't take the job. I think you will."

"Why?"

"It's a puzzle. I've heard you like to solve puzzles. Of course the other factor is that your gun is going to be extremely important in this matter. These are desperate men who have in their hands land patents that could be worth a hundred million dollars in say twenty years."

"That much?"

"It could be ten times that much, depending on the speed of development on and near that land here in Nebraska. Now the land is sold for from $2 to $7 an acre. In fifty years the same land will be worth three-thousand dollars an acre. I'm not fast at multiplication, Mr. Morgan, but the sum is staggering."

Morgan lifted his brows.

"Yes indeed, Mr. Morgan, a tidy sum."

Morgan scratched the back of his neck and looked at Johnson. "Since you're still trying to find the paper, that must mean no one has cashed in on it yet. Wouldn't there have to be a forgery and a registration of deed at the county courthouse?"

"Right. We think the patent deeds are lost somewhere around North Platte, Nebraska. Perhaps the thieves had a falling out, or one got killed. They might even have been lost and destroyed. Either way, we need to know."

"Can't the patent deeds be replaced if they're lost?" Morgan asked.

"My legal people say they can. But we'd have to present a lot of evidence of what happened. We don't have that. Besides, I'd have to go back to Senator Perridale, the Nebraska hot shot, and I don't want to deal with that man.

"It could bring up a whole legal tangle that I don't want to get into right now. It also could take another six months. I have buyers that I need to get revenue from for a lot of this land. I want to find the patents so I don't have to go through that."

Morgan sipped at his drink. Johnson lit a long brown cigar.

"One thing I don't understand," Morgan said. "If these papers are not like paper money, what good are they to the thieves who stole them?"

"Ransom. My first thought was that they were being held until we paid a ransom for them."

"But nobody contacted you. Seems reasonable they're lost. I'm not sure I want to play this kind of a game."

Johnson walked over to where Morgan stood by the window.

"Look, fast gun, don't try anything with me. I know your reputation. I also know you're damned hard to deal with, that you aren't always on the right side of the law and that you're still wanted in two states. If you're trying to jack up the price, it won't work. I can buy a lot of lawyers for ten-thousand dollars."

Lee reached for his brown hat with the red diamonds on the black headband. "Peers that I'll have to think it over for a spell."

"How long?"

"A week or so."

"Oh, one more thing I forgot to tell you. That courier, a man named Kasper Gorman, the one who had the satchel locked to his wrist. The robbers took him with them for a while. Then they chopped his hand off at the wrist so they could get the chain off him. Then they killed the courier. But they did it after they cut off his hand. Nice gents you have out there in North Platte."

Morgan twisted his hat in his hands. "How

much did your lawyers tell you the robbers might ask for the return of the goods?" Morgan asked.

"In the satchel were patent deeds for two of the twenty mile lengths of track laid and approved. How much do you think a quarter-of-a-million acres of Nebraska farm and ranchland is worth?"

Morgan shrugged.

"I told you, right now it's selling for from $2 to $7 an acre, depending on water. Three-dollars average, at a half million acres, is one and a half dollars. Right now!"

"Any respectable thief would want twenty percent," Morgan said. "That's three hundred thousand. I'd be a bargain at twenty thousand." Morgan walked to the door and looked back.

"Goddamn!" Johnson said. He threw up his hands in defeat. "Done, twenty thousand." He glanced up at Morgan with his eyes so light blue they were almost white. "You've held me up once on this deal, don't try to do it twice."

Morgan walked back into the room. "I'll need five hundred dollars in expense money and the names of all of your people in that area who might have been involved. I especially want the names of the men who would *know* that the papers were coming through by courier."

Morgan saw one of the men leave the room quietly. Morgan walked to the big desk and picked up an ivory paperweight.

"I want the reports of Pinkerton and the sheriff and the names of any suspects that you might have. I need to know if you have any railroad detectives working on the case and if so, who they are and what they have turned up. In short, I want to know everything you know about this robbery before I get back on the train." Morgan grinned. "Oh, yeah, and I want a lifetime pass on the Union Pacific for two, signed by your hand."

"Goddamn, Morgan, you better be good. Part of this isn't the money, you realize that. I just can't have people robbing me this way and getting away with it. If I don't stop it now, it will get bigger and bigger like a snowball rolling downhill on a sunny winter day."

The man came back in the room with an envelope. He gave it to Johnson who looked inside, then gave it to Morgan. Inside were a sheaf of greenbacks and eight twenty-dollar gold pieces.

Morgan sat down in the chair and grinned. "Now for those reports so I'll have something to do tonight while I wait for the train to leave in the morning."

The reports, an inch thick stack of papers, were ready in another large envelope that had been put into a leather case.

Morgan put on his low crowned hat, touched the brim and walked outside looking for a good restaurant. He was starved.

That night in his hotel room he read through the papers. He found several interesting facts.

The courier delivering the patent deeds had indeed been killed and mutilated and his hand never found. The killing was unsolved in Lincoln county. These particular grant deeds had been written in 20 section lots, so there were 40 individual patents issued and enclosed in the satchel.

The satchel itself was of brown cowhide leather about ten inches wide, a foot long and six inches high. It had a pair of sturdy handles and opened from the top to each side. It was held closed by two railroad padlocks. There was a drawing of the satchel.

This was standard procedure for delivering land grant deeds to the county of record rail office.

The Pinkerton report was long but said little. They had assigned six agents to the case, two working along the line and four in North Platte. The report detailed activities of two men, one Ben Allison, a gambler of sorts who was known to move from town to town, and Shorty Wilberton. Wilberton vanished shortly after the robbery and had not been seen in town since.

Wilberton was described as a drifter and saloon fixture who usually was broke so cadged drinks. He was in his thirties, worked now and again as a cowboy or farm hand. He was wanted for questioning by the Sheriff since he had been seen leading a spare horse toward the area where the train was stopped.

Pinkerton also gave an account of the robbery "so far as is known:

"The regular passenger and freight train left the station at Kearney, Nebraska on time, experienced no problems or unforeseen events. There were no unruly passengers or violence of any kind on the two passenger cars. The courier, Kasper Gorman, 29, had been with the company since its inception.

"The courier rode in the express car since it carried the mail and a safe and was considered secure and protected.

"A mile outside of North Platte, a man appeared on the tracks dressed in trainman's blue striped overalls and blue railroad cap waving a red flag to stop the train. This is known as a flag stop and is generally accepted procedure for the railroads.

"The engineer reported he feared there was trouble in North Platte or perhaps the river had washed out the tracks again. He stopped the train.

"At once, the express car was entered by two men with masks over their faces and drawn revolvers. One was probably the man who stopped the train since he also wore railroad striped overalls. There was no thought of danger by the express man on board and his firearms were all in a drawer.

"Without speaking a word, the two desperados hustled Gorman off the train. The courier was forced to run with the two others to a patch of brush 30 yards away. There three horses waited. Gorman was made to mount a horse. By then the express man got out his rifle and fired two shots at the departing riders, but they were out of any effective range for the express man who said: 'I am no marksman with a rifle.'

"The train started up and continued to North Platte where the incident was reported to the county sheriff who mounted six men and made an immediate search and planned to give chase. Later Sheriff Emery Lewis reported that he found some horse tracks at the site, but they were soon lost in a hundred others on the River Road close by and the desperados could not be followed.

"A week later a body was found about ten miles north of town by a pair of pheasant hunters. They brought it to the sheriff where it was identified by railroad officials as that of Kasper Gorman, the courier. Gorman's left hand had been removed above the wrist. The amputation was not surgical and appeared to be done with a large sharp instrument such as an axe.

"Gorman's body was transported to Illinois for burial."

There were a dozen more pages reporting what the Pinkerton men did in North Platte, who they talked to, and what they found out, but none of it had led to any discoveries or the identification of either of the hold up men.

Morgan threw down the papers in disgust. He wasn't a damn detective. If Pinkerton used six men for six months and couldn't find a clue, why was he taking on the job?

He snorted. At last he shrugged. Hell, he had 20,000 good reasons to take the job and they all had dollar signs on them. He stuffed the papers back in the big envelope. He'd done more reading tonight than he had in the last two years. Now he wanted to rest his eyes.

Morgan had the pass in his pocket and a date with an 8 A.M. passenger train leaving the Omaha Southern Pacific station. He didn't want to miss the train.

Chapter Three

Morgan came away from where he had been leaning against the store front on this warm sunny day in North Platte. In town two hours and his first contact got himself killed right in front of Morgan's eyes.

The courier kidnapped, mutilated and now dead and buried.

The drifter seen with a spare horse in the robbery area vanished.

Who was now his contact in town? Local, or just in for the job?

He had almost nothing to go with. Hell, he'd start from the beginning.

Ten minutes later he had rented a horse from the livery stable, thrown on a saddle and began his ride out a mile to the east of town along the tracks where the train had been stopped and the robbery taken place. Kidnapping, too. Murder later. All for some damn pieces of paper?

Absolutely, when the papers meant land, good land that eventually would be worth hundreds of millions of dollars.

Nebraska is a plains state, flat, unending, much unwatered. A mile out of North Platte there were no rapids in the gentle flow of the stream. Some describe the Platte River as a waterway that is up to a half mile wide in spots, and a half inch deep. Morgan had heard all the stories about Nebraska, but this was an up close look.

He nudged the bay closer to the tracks and found what he was hunting, a 4x4 post planted deep in the right of way with a red X painted on it. That was the place the train engineer had been suckered into stopping.

As Morgan figured, there was nothing else here. Part of the right of way had been trampled down by horses where a posse had moved in and out six months ago. According to the report, the robbers had hidden their horses in the brush along a small feeder stream that emptied nearby into the Platte River.

Morgan checked the brush, knowing he wouldn't find anything there. He didn't at first but since he was already there, Morgan stepped off the bay and let her search for some stray grass as he walked around. There were still horse droppings in the grass, which meant the animals had stayed there for a while waiting for the train to come. He found a bit of leather which could have dropped off a harness strap or part of a bridle. Not a chance to identify it or match it with any tack.

He took a step backward and stepped on something which almost caused him to fall down. A rock? He looked down and pushed some dry grass aside and found what looked like a child's wooden block. He picked it up. It was maybe a half-inch thick and three-inches long by two-inches wide.

Strange. It seemed to be well finished, or oiled, had a lot of small nicks and some gouges in it and some black stains. He was about to throw it away, then he tossed it into the air and caught it. He slid the block into his pocket.

Nothing else of any value seemed to be there. The block probably was useless, but he was working with nothing. You just never could tell.

Lee Morgan mounted and rode the route witnesses reported seeing the robbers take as the train slowly pulled away from its stop. The trail soon hit the old stage road from Kearney to North Platte. It still got lots of use by local farmers and ranchers.

Now, as the sheriff must have six months ago, Morgan found the dirt roadway full of horse and wheel tracks. Impossible to track anyone on this roadway. The robbers had been heading back for town, but as the train caught up with them and then passed them, the three horsemen turned off the road north and continued until the witness on the train could no longer see them.

They rode at least ten miles out because that's where they found the courier's body. Did they carry an axe with them all that way simply to chop off the man's hand? Maybe they stole it from a farm along the way. He might never know.

Morgan rode back into town and put the horse in the livery, then talked to the agent at the Union Pacific station.

"Hell yes, I remember that day. Biggest excitement we've had around here in six months. The Zephyr got stopped about a mile out and two armed men pulled off some courier. Big money involved, I hear."

"Who did it?" Morgan asked.

The agent, a man in his forties, burst out laughing. He wiped tears from his eyes. "Land o'goshen. If I knew that right now I wouldn't be here. I'd be spending me a thousand dollar reward. Company has been asking everybody about that one."

"Who could have known the man would be on the train," Morgan asked. As he did he took out the printed card that was embossed with the seal of Union Pacific and signed by Quenton Johnson himself. He handed the lifetime pass for two to the trainman.

"Land o'goshen, look at that! Old Johnson himself, huh? Glory be. You must be somebody. You asked who would know the courier was coming? Half a dozen people, I'd guess. Most of them from Omaha. I'd seen him before, and I knew what he carried. Hard to miss with that chain locked around his wrist that way. It was like saying, 'Hey, I've got important stuff here.' "

"So even if I knew the men's names, it wouldn't help me much?"

"About the size of it. A couple of vice presidents, the treasurer, those kinds."

"Have couriers come through since?"

"Oh, sure. I can spot them. They aren't so obvious now, but I can tell. Don't use the chain anymore, smaller case, more like business people carry. And now they have a hidden gun on them."

Morgan thanked him and walked through town to the newspaper office. He found it on a siding. The old box car had the sliding doors open and a set of wooden steps built up to the rail car level. Morgan walked up. He'd read a report about the newspaper and the owner, one Lame Charlie Bard.

When Morgan came to the top of the steps he found a small open area, and counters cutting off both ends of the rail car. On one side was a desk and some file areas and storage shelves. Stacks of paper filled half the area.

A young man looked up. He had spectacles, had

been working on a pad of writing paper. His pencil still poised over the story he wrote.

"Yes, good afternoon. Help you?"

"Charlie Bard?"

"I must be getting famous, you knew me right away." He laughed and stood, then came up to the counter. His left knee didn't work and he dragged his leg just a little.

"Mr. Bard, I'm here looking into the problem of the missing patent deeds owned by the railroad. You ran several stories on the loss about six months ago."

"Oh, yeah, the million dollar swindle. It was big news for a while, especially when they found that courier's body with one hand gone, for God's sakes. Nothing's happened to rate an inch of type since then, though. I hear the railroad fired the Pinkerton team of detectives. You the new hired man?"

"You could say that, but not very loud." It wasn't a threat but Morgan's voice had gone flat, low and with a steel in it that made a man stop and chose his words carefully.

"Look, I didn't mean anything. Mind if I do a small story about you?"

"You do and you'll be looking around to find your head," Morgan said in the same flat, deadly tone of voice. "I'm not here looking for newspaper stories about me. I want to read what you wrote about the problem six months ago."

Lame Charlie Bard seemed to shrink about an inch in height as he watched Morgan. He nodded. "Yes, sir, no trouble. I have the clips right here in my morgue."

He went to a drawer at the side of the long narrow room and brought back a folder full of clips.

"Everything I've written about the story is inside. Oh, I didn't get your name."

"Morgan, Lee Morgan, and I don't want to see it in print, not ever."

Lame Charlie nodded and limped back to his desk as Morgan read the clippings. They were neatly arranged by date in chronological order.

The news stories were factual, straight, well written and clear. Lame Charlie seemed to be a good news reporter. Morgan read every word critically, but he could discover no new slant, find no new suspect. He carried the envelope back to Lame Charlie who had switched sides of the box car.

Now he had on a printer's apron and a composing stick in his hand working over a type case setting up a story one letter at a time from the moveable type.

Morgan watched him a minute.

"Every letter goes in one at a time?" Morgan asked.

"Until I invent this machine I'm working on to do the job. I've got this idea to do it with a gravity feed by hitting a bar for each different letter and it would fall down this little slot and go into a stick and that would then he lifted out and pressed into a form where liquid lead would be forced into. . . ."

Lame Charlie looked up and grinned. "Everybody says I'm crazy to even think about it, but it can be done. I know it can."

He set an inch of lines of type in a metal "stick" down on a marble topped table and adjusted more type in a rectangular metal form that was big enough to hold a whole page of a newspaper. Part of it was filled with type.

Some of it was in large letters. The headlines, Morgan decided. Some of it was empty and in places there were bars standing at type height. Those would be the rules, the lines between the newspaper columns. Morgan decided he'd spend more time looking at the next newspaper he saw.

"This is the side of the paper I like best," Lame Charlie said. "Of course it has to be written and the advertisements sold, before I can work over here."

Morgan stood there a minute, put the envelope down on the counter and waved. "Remember, nothing in the paper. Might be best if you forgot I even came in and talked."

Lame Charlie looked up from another type case. This one seemed to have large letters an inch high or more.

"Those made of metal, too?" Morgan asked.

"Not these big ones, they're wood type, one-inch to three-inch are almost always wood."

Morgan waved again and went out of the rail car and down the steps. He moved back the short block to the main street and looked up and down.

He was registered in the only frame hotel in town, a two story affair half a block down, The Nebraskan. It couldn't have more than twenty rooms, total. Just so his room had a bed.

The sun was threatening to quit for the day so maybe he should, as well. He turned to go back to his hotel when he slammed into someone. A woman in a long blue print dress and a small blue hat jolted away from him, lost her balance and sat down hard on the boardwalk.

Morgan caught his balance and reached down for her hand.

"Ma'am, I'm sorry. I wasn't watching my trail well enough."

The woman who sat there shook her head as if to clear it from the tumble. She was young and blonde and now a hint of anger faded from her features as she held up her hand to Morgan.

As he lifted her to her feet, he saw dimples dent

her soft white cheeks and a flash of her brown eyes with flecks of gold in them. When he set her on her feet he saw she was about five-three, and the blue dress touched the boardwalk, but couldn't hide her slender waist and big breasts.

"Mercy me, I was the one wasn't looking where I was going," she said, not trying to hide a slight southern twang to her talk.

"Miss, it was my fault. I changed directions too quickly. Are you all right?"

"My goodness, just dropped me on the seat of my pants. I'm fine. I'm tougher than you might think."

"Are you sure? Any spots in front of your eyes?"

She giggled. "I usually don't see spots."

"Let me take you into the restaurant and get you some coffee or something so you can recover."

"I'm fine, just fine." She looked at him evenly and then a slight smile tinged her features. "Well, I guess that would be all right. But we must be introduced. My name is Willa Porterfield and I'm from Atlanta, but more recently from Omaha."

"Miss Porterfield, it's a pleasure to meet you. I'm Lee Morgan and right now this is my town. I move around the west quite a bit."

"Nice to meet you, Mr. Morgan. I hear they have some of that new iced cream in the hotel restaurant. Can we try some? I never have had any."

"Of course." Morgan took her arm and led the way down the boardwalk and half block to the hotel, The Nebraskan. She was an extremely pretty girl, the blonde hair around her shoulders, the saucy little way she smiled, and those dimples. Morgan had always been a pushover for a woman with dimples in both cheeks.

"Iced cream?" he asked. "What's that?"

"I'm not sure. It's so new not many places have

it. They make it out of cream and eggs and sugar and some flavoring and maybe fruits or berries, all sorts of good things, and then mix it up and freeze it while stirring and it comes out just wonderful, I'm told."

Inside the hotel they went directly to the dining room and found a table next to the wall. They ordered the iced cream and waited.

"Have you been in town long?" she asked him.

"Just arrived today, fact is, from Omaha. What about you?"

"Oh, I've been here on and off for three or four months."

They talked of other things as people do who are just getting acquainted and soon the dishes of iced cream arrived. Today was strawberry day, the waitress told them. The ice cream was piled in a round dish with a stem on it. The concoction was not really frozen, rather it was thick and creamy and with fresh strawberries mixed in it.

Willa tried a taste and her gold flecked brown eyes glowed with pleasure.

"Oh, it's delicious. I'm never going to eat anything else for as long as I live!"

Morgan tried it, then had a spoonful and he agreed. "It is good, especially on a hot day. I wonder how they make it?"

"Somebody told me there was a machine with a handle and you put crushed ice around the inside and then put the tank in it and put salt on the ice and then turn the handle of the crank, and all sorts of things."

They talked little then and ate the iced cream.

"Are you staying here in the hotel?" he asked.

"Why, yes. I'm in town to see an old friend, but she has a small little house."

"I'm staying here, too. Now that we've had our desert, would you like to order dinner? It's almost time."

"Oh, my goodness is it that late? Oh, well, I'll do the shopping tomorrow. Yes, dinner would be a fine idea."

They ate and talked and he was more intrigued by her than before. She was a delightful companion and so pretty he was amazed.

"What are you doing in town?" she asked.

"Land. I'm looking for some land to buy for a group in Omaha who think this section of the state is going to boom now that the railroad is through here. I think they're right."

Dinner was over and they lingered over coffee. At last even that was gone.

She stretched and he was afraid the bodice of her dress might come apart from the pressure of her breasts.

"Well, Mr. Morgan, it has been delightful. Now it's time for me to go up to my room and write some letters. My old mother in Atlanta still worries about me."

He stood and held her chair. "At least I can walk you up to your room. What number?"

"I always get room 211, it brings me good luck."

"That's a gambler's number."

"Sometimes I gamble a little," she said smiling.

At her door he took her hand gently. "I'm glad I ran into you today, Willa Porterfield. Maybe we'll meet again."

"I hope so. This isn't such a big place." She smiled.

"Not large at all, and with me in room 210 just across the hall we'll have lots of chances to meet again."

She laughed, reached up and kissed his cheek, then stepped quickly into her room. When she closed the door, he heard the bolt slip into place.

Morgan lifted his brows, then grinned. There was always tomorrow, little lady, he thought. He knew he would be seeing more of Willa Porterfield. All of her, he hoped.

Chapter Four

That night Morgan re-read about half of the report by the Pinkerton detectives and the express man on the rail car. It didn't help. He still had a lot of nothing to go on. No names, no suspects, nothing.

Hell, he was no damn detective. Give him a man to hunt down and he'd find him. This was like hunting for a dandelion in a clover field. Tomorrow he'd send a telegram to Johnson that he was quitting. He'd give them back the rest of the five hundred and use his pass to get back to Denver. He'd keep the pass.

From long habit, Morgan pushed a straight backed chair under the door knob to his room, hoisting it up on the back legs and wedging it in firmly. Anybody trying to come in would have to break the chair and that would cause one hell of a racket.

He looked down at the street from the darkened

window for a moment after he blew out the kerosene lamp. He was on the second story, so it would be harder for anyone to break in. Not that he expected anyone, but he had lived this long by not taking any more chances than were necessary.

The moon was out. Morgan pushed the window down and locked it, then crawled into bed. He slept at once.

Later, Morgan wasn't sure how long, he heard a bump on the outside of the wall. He was awake in an instant. In his business waking up fast and ready to fight had saved his scalp more than once.

He rolled out of bed and looked at the window. The bump had been on that wall. An instant later he saw a shadow outside the window, then something came crashing through the glass.

Morgan had his Bisley Colts up and almost fired before he saw it wasn't a man. It had to be something tied on a rope and swung from the roof. Whoever swung it missed the first time. That was the bump against the wall.

Morgan looked at the gift on the floor in the moonlight. At the same time he smelled smoke and saw the sputtering end of a dynamite fuse. The burning section was still two feet away from the cap and powder.

Morgan grabbed his knife, cut the rope in half near the bomb and threw the four sticks of dynamite out the window. The bomb landed in a wagon parked below in the street. A few seconds later the dynamite went off with a cracking roar.

By that time Morgan had slid into his boots, strapped on his gunbelt and bolted out his door for the stairs leading up to the roof. He came to the door, saw a lock and smashed into the panel with his shoulder.

Weakened wood splintered and he came out on the tar paper roof. He saw a white hat go over the side and down a steel ladder on the back of the two story structure. Morgan beat down the urge to shoot the bushwhacker off the ladder. Instead, he holstered his six-gun and hurried down the ladder after the man.

He went down like the firemen do, sliding his hands along the outside of the ladder and letting his feet slip from rung to rung. That way he covered twice the distance in the usual time. He was six feet from the ground when he slammed into the slow moving man on the ladder below him.

The man screeched as he fell off and dropped the last six feet to the ground.

Morgan followed right beside him and kicked the six-gun out of the man's trembling hand.

Morgan stood him up and slammed a quick left and then a right fist into his face before the surprised gunman could defend himself. He jolted backwards against the hotel wall where Morgan caught him and powered two fists into the man's belly. The bomber gagged and bent over to relieve the pain.

Lee rammed his right knee upward, caught the man's chin and snapped is head back, dumping him into the alley half unconscious. It took a half dozen slaps across his face to bring the man back to the talking stage.

"Why did you swing that bomb into my room?" Morgan demanded, holding one hand loosely around the man's throat. He gurgled and Morgan eased the pressure.

"Damn, not my idea. Some gent paid me."

"Who, damn you! Who paid you to kill me?"

"Dunno. Never saw him plain. Just some gent outside the saloon. It was dark. Wore a suit, hat, necktie. Gave me ten dollars and the bomb and the rope. All I had to do. . . ."

Morgan hit him again with his fist, loosened a

tooth, brought a spout of blood from his nose and smashed his head back to the alley dirt.

"Christ, don't!" the man pleaded.

Morgan had cocked his Colt and laid the muzzle against the man's forehead.

"Why not? You tried to kill me. Turn about is fair play. Now it's my turn to try to kill you. Think I can win the contest?"

"I got a wife . . . and a daughter. . . ."

"Should have thought about them before you tried to become a killer. Who paid you? Give me a name or you're dead."

"Charlie, Charlie Bard."

Morgan snorted. "First name you could think of, right? He's the newspaper editor and publisher. He probably doesn't even own a black fancy suit."

Morgan eased to his feet, the gun still covering the man.

"Stand up, killer."

The bushwhacker struggled to get up. Morgan slid his weapon back in leather and moved forward with his fists, mashing the man's face into a bloody mess, knocking him down, picking him up. He felt good as he smashed another tooth loose in the bomber's jaw. Morgan knew his hands would be sore and battered tomorrow.

The man went down again, and Morgan left him there.

"Bastard, I should kill you. I'm getting soft." He kicked the man hard in the side and he rolled over groaning. Morgan kicked him once more, then found the man's six-gun and stripped the rounds from it and threw it on top of the hotel's roof.

He walked down to the hotel's side door and went up to his room. Who knew he was here and wanted him dead? He didn't know. He washed off his bloody hands, bathed them in some witch hazel and bay rum he carried in his carpetbag and then packed his gear. He checked doors until he found a room not occupied. He moved in there and braced the door again, then fell on the bed.

Now he had another problem. Tomorrow he'd start working on it as well. No, tomorrow he was quitting this railroad job.

Morgan laughed softly. He wasn't quitting, not now. Not when some asshole tried to blow him into dime sized chunks with a four stick dynamite bomb. Somebody just made his first mistake, and Morgan would be there to help him make the last one he would make in this world.

In spite of his late night, Morgan woke up at six A.M. and couldn't get back to sleep. His hands hurt. He soaked them in cold water from the crockery pitcher which he poured in the wash basin. It helped. Then he washed his face and torso, shaved in cold water, put on a clean shirt and a pair of town pants, and a soft doeskin vest and went out looking for breakfast.

Across the street and half a block down he saw a sign that said "Marleen's Cafe." A sign in the window said "Breakfast served from 6:30 A.M." He walked down and looked in the window. It was small, bright and cheery, just the kind of eatery he liked.

A tinkling bell rang as he walked in. There were six tables and a counter where eight more people could sit. He saw nobody who seemed to work there. Two men sat at the counter drinking coffee. A man at one of the tables worked on a large plate filled with eggs and country fried potatoes.

He sat down at the counter.

"Marleen'll be here in a minute," one of the men nursing his coffee said.

Morgan nodded and waited. If the customers help out it must be a good place to eat.

A moment later, a young woman came through

the door that led into the back room and stopped in front of Morgan.

"Coffee to start?" she asked.

Morgan knew he was grinning. He did that sometimes around women he was impressed by. Marleen smiled back. She was tall and slender, maybe five-six, with dark hair cut short and close around her face. She had dark brows and light green eyes that were set far apart in an oval face. There were no dimples but a snub of a nose and a mouth that was too large but only made her smile wider, more appealing.

"Are we just going to have this grinning contest or can I take your order?" she asked. Then she laughed and both the coffee drinkers chuckled, too.

Morgan got his senses back and nodded. "Yes, coffee."

"And. . . ."

"Three eggs sunny side up, lots of bacon, some of those country fries, toast and some jam. Be enough for a start."

She didn't write anything down, just nodded, winked at the next man down the counter. "Be right out with your victuals, Irv. Keep working on that coffee."

She vanished into the back where the kitchen must be. The man nearest him, Irv, looked at Morgan and smiled.

"Ain't she something? I ask her to marry me every morning. Some damn young pisser gonna come along and grab her one of these days. I'd give five thousand dollars right now to be twenty years younger."

Marleen swept out, put a cup of coffee down in front of Morgan without sloshing out a drop and scooted back to the kitchen before any of the men could say a word.

Morgan looked over at Irv. "She's not married?"

"Was. She and her new husband just bought a
ranch out about fifteen miles. Sioux renegades
came charging through one day. Killed him and
their one ranch hand, took all the horses, shot up
the cattle and burned down every building on the
place. Marleen had been out riding fence looking
for a break. She came back to death and des-
truction."

Irv stopped talking quickly as Marleen came in
with a big platter of breakfast and a little tray
with three kinds of jam on it in family style crocks.

She put them down in front of Irv, patted his
hand.

"You eat slow, there's no cause to rush and get
the pains again." She looked over at Morgan.
"More coffee?"

He nodded. She came back with a heavy metal
pot. She poured Morgan's cup full then set the pot
down on a hot pad on the counter.

"Irv, if that java starts to get cold, you tell me."
She looked at Morgan. "Mister, have your breakfast in a minute." She was gone again.

Irv concentrated on eating. Two more men came
in and sat at a table at the far end. Morgan felt as if
he should help her serve them. He snorted. Where
did that feeling come from.

A half hour later he had eaten his biggest breakfast in a long time. Everything was good, great.
The jam was home made, strawberry, apple butter
and wild plum. Morgan worked on another cup of
coffee. Only he and the two men at the far table
were still there.

Marleen came out and sat at the end of the
counter two chairs down from Morgan and sipped
at a small cup of coffee.

"Best breakfast I've had in years," Morgan said.

Marleen looked up, blushed a little and nodded.
"Thanks. You must not have any home
cooking . . . at home."

"You're right. My name's Lee Morgan. You're Marleen?"

"Yes, Mr. Morgan, Mrs. Marleen Forrester."

"I heard about your ranch . . . I'm sorry."

"Life goes on . . . for the living."

He watched her.

"More coffee, Mr. Morgan?"

He shook his head.

"I better get back to work." A sign said breakfast was thirty cents. He left her a silver fifty cent piece.

Lee stood. "See you this noon," he said and walked out as she turned and watched him, a small smile touching her pretty face.

Chapter Five

Out on the street after breakfast, Morgan headed for the bank. It was the only brick building in town, not so big, but solid and confident-looking among the tents and occasional frame building.

He was almost there when a man called his name from behind. Morgan turned slowly, his right hand hanging at his side ready for whatever developed.

A small man in a Western shirt, blue jeans and a cowboy hat walked up and nodded.

"You are Lee Morgan, aren't you?" the man asked. He was about five-six, on the slight side, with dark hair, a firm nose and darting black eyes. He wore a moustache and long sideburns that hadn't quite filled out yet.

"Yep, I'm Morgan."

"Good, my name is Alexis Savage and I need to have a talk with you. Can I buy you a beer?"

"Too early for me. How about a sit down?" Morgan pointed to a pair of wooden chairs outside the Platte General Store. They were for the convenience of the store's customers, but anybody who wanted to could use them.

The two men sat down and Savage lit up a thin, black cigar. He offered one to Morgan who shook his head.

"Mr. Morgan, I know who you are and that you're here working for the railroad. You're trying to find out what happened to those patent deeds issued to the Union Pacific for almost a half million acres of land grant property."

"So?"

"It's a tough assignment. I want to help you. I have certain information and facts that will take you weeks to dig up."

"How come you know all this about the problem?"

"Because I'm a former Pinkerton detective and I worked for almost four months on this case before we were dismissed."

"I heard you all were fired. Why would you want to help me earn my pay from the railroad?"

Alexis smiled. "I'm not being generous, I'm afraid. Those documents have a real cash value . . . a good price can be negotiated for their return. All we have to do is find them, let Union Pacific pay the ransom for their return, split the cash and be rich men for the rest of our lives."

Morgan lowered his hat with the red diamonds on it over his face until it covered his eyes, then he leaned back in the chair. "Seems to me that's what the gents had in mind who stole the papers in the first place. Didn't work out none too good for them."

"They were stupid, bungling, idiots. A pair of smart men, teamed up with my background on the case and your talents with your gun, could produce entirely different results."

"Why would I turn against my employer and give up a handsome fee for finding the papers?"

"Because we could get a hundred thousand dollars for the goods, from the railroad. I'd wager they didn't offer you that much to bring them back."

"True," Morgan said from under his hat. He watched the small man through a slit between felt and skin. "But I hired on, gave my pledge. . . ."

Savage chuckled. "Ah, yes, the pledge of a man wanted by the law in three states. A man who has in the past not been overly particular about who he signed on with to use his gun for. Mr. Morgan, pardon me for saying so, but your reputation is not that of a man who is overly careful about the law, with justice, or with the truth. At least that's what your reputation is." He added the last thought quickly.

Morgan made no move. "Those wanted posters are all misunderstandings. It was self defense. My defense was simply better than the other guys'."

"Perhaps. I've seen situations like that. But I've also seen a lot of this town and its people and know a lot about what happened that day the patent deeds were stolen. You probably have a copy of our report. Of course, one hell of a lot of what I know never went into our report."

"Such as what?" Morgan asked.

"I'll tell you all I know as soon as we shake hands on our new partnership."

"I'll do some thinking on it," Morgan said. He pushed his hat up and stared at Savage. "Do you have a black suit and a white shirt?"

"I do. Not a new suit, but it's black."

"Oh."

"Why do you ask?"

"Do you know how to use dynamite?"

Savage chuckled. "Mr. Morgan. I did not send that dynamite bomb swinging into your hotel room last night. I did hear about it, however, as did the sheriff and half of the town. The lawman is looking for somebody to pay for the ruined wagon. No, I didn't try to kill you last night."

"Good," Morgan said and pulled the hat down over his eyes and leaned the chair against the wall so it rested on just the back legs.

"How long will you need to think over our partnership?"

"Day or two. I'm on no kind of schedule."

"Whoever tried for you last night will give it another go-round."

"True."

"A gun at your back might be helpful."

"Might."

Savage stood. "You do your thinking, I'll be around."

Morgan watched the small man walk down the street and go into a tent top saloon. This was becoming more interesting. If Savage was hunting for the documents on his own, it must mean he knew for sure that they had not been destroyed or totally lost down a mine shaft or washed down the river.

Things were starting to develop. Another player in the game. Johnson must have some people here working for him. So far none of them had surfaced. With stakes this high there could be several railroad men keeping tabs on things here. At least one of them must be watching him. Good enough.

He pushed away from the wall, let the chair land on all four legs, got up and walked down the street. He was wasting his time here. He had to go see the educated Indian, his last lead. A Sioux with a college degree who had come back to the tribe to try to help his people adjust to the white man's way of living.

The suggestion from the railroad people was that the Sioux tribe living in scattered bands to the north, might know something about the affair. They might have seen the two white men, might have contacted the Sioux, might know who the men were or where they went. It was a wild goose chase lead, but the last one he could work.

Morgan went to the Nebraskan Hotel to change into riding clothes. He stopped at the desk and told the clerk he'd changed rooms last night after the window was broken. He was now in room 216 and wanted the key. The clerk gave it to him with only a mumbled apology about the broken window.

"Don't show on your books which room I have," Morgan said with a touch of raw steel in his voice. "I'd just as soon not have any more visitors like the one last night." The clerk nodded, crossed out the room number and handed him the key.

Upstairs at room 216, he pushed the key into the lock and saw the door edge forward, unlocked, unlatched. The Colt came into his right hand in a fraction of a second and he kicked the door open, the Colt covering the room.

She sat on his bed and looked up quickly, long blonde hair swirling, coming off her shoulders and covering one side of her chest. Nothing covered the other side where one large breast glowed all white and pink the nipple already extended, dark red with hot blood.

"Hi, wondered when you would come back," Willa Porterfield said, a big smile on her face.

Morgan never lost a beat. He continued inside, holstered his weapon and closed the door. He locked it, slid in the bolt and then put a chair under the door knob.

When he turned back to the bed, Willa had moved up on her knees, her legs slightly spread, her hair all back over her shoulders and her whole body naked, ready, inviting him. He walked to the bed, leaned down and kissed both her breasts, then her lips.

She let out a long sigh.

"Oh, good! I was afraid there for a moment . . ."

Morgan sat on the bed and kissed her breast again, gentle soft kisses circling around and around it until he reached the peak where he bit her nipple softly before he sucked most of the orb into his mouth and chewed on it.

"Oh, darling yes!" she crooned. "That feels so delicious, so marvelous. Do you mind if I talk? I love to talk during love making, to tell you exactly how I'm feeling."

"I'd like that," Morgan said as he switched from one side to the other giving the second breast the same oral treatment.

"Oh, God, but I'm melting! I need to lay down." She caught his shoulders and brought him with her as she lay backward on the big bed. He covered half of her with his body.

"Touch me just all over!" she said softly. "I want you to touch me everywhere, every way you can. Right now, darling. Then I'll undress you and return the favor. I'm so hot and ready from just undressing and waiting for you.

"Somebody told me once that thinking about all the sexy, wonderful fun you're going to have is half the thrill of making love. Do you think that's true?"

His lips had moved up to her throat. He licked soft white skin and she shivered. When he got to her mouth she opened it wide and he drove his tongue inside deeply until she writhed on the bed in total joy.

Then he left that opening and kissed her eyes, up across her forehead and down to one ear. His tongue washed the inside of her ear and she moaned in rapture.

"Do that again, again! I'm going to climax. I can't . . . I can't hold back any more!" Then her whole body shook under him and he lifted off her but she pulled him down, rough clothes and all, on top of her as her hips slammed upward against his and her body rattled and spasmed with vibrations that excited Morgan the way few things could.

Beads of sweat formed on her brow as she rumbled once more and then dissolved into a lump of flesh on the mattress. He licked the sweat off her forehead and she looked up and grabbed him and kissed him furiously.

She rolled him over and began to tear at his clothes. He helped.

"Oh, Christ but that was wonderful! How can you do it? I've never cum that way when somebody licked my ear." She scowled for a moment, then grinned. "I guess I figured you were fucking me in the ear and I wanted to catch up."

She pulled his vest off and his shirt, kissed his man nipples and watched them respond. "Good, chest hair. I love a man with lots of hair on his body. It means he's going to be a wild animal when he gets it inside of me."

She concentrated then on the buttons on his town pants, at last got the system, and opened them all. She rubbed the hardness, the large lump behind his short underwear. Eagerly she pushed the underwear aside and lifted his penis.

"It works! Glory be. I hate it when I get a big build up and then a man's thing won't get hard. Glory, what a good one!"

She bent and kissed the turgid head and watched it surge upward in anticipation.

Willa jumped off the bed and pulled at his trousers, then the short underwear until he was naked.

"That's better," she said looking at him. "God but a man is so beautiful! Big shoulders and a flat belly and narrow waist and hips and . . . oh lord, the best part, his cock!" She knelt in front of him and gulped half of his tool into her mouth in one bite and bounded up and down a dozen times, then came off it and rolled on the bed.

"Now, if you could do anything you wanted to with me right now, what would it be?"

Morgan looked down at her sleek young form, so appetizing, so delicious. "I'd smear iced cream all over you and eat you with a big spoon."

She giggled, then laughed and jumped up and kissed him.

"Good, good, now something a little more practical, a little more hot sexy wild!"

"Stand up," he told her.

"I can't do it standing up, I'm built too far back or something. That's what somebody told me."

She stood on the floor and and spread her legs. Morgan bent and crouched and lifted and Willa shrieked.

"Oh, lordy, I can do it standing up! He was the one who couldn't."

"Lock your ankles behind my back," Morgan told her. She giggled, but got it done then laced her fingers together behind his neck.

He moved with them still locked together to the wall. "We could go out in the hallway."

She giggled again. "Then we can charge the people a dollar each to watch!"

They both laughed. He pushed her back against the wall and began stroking.

"Lordy that's . . . that's so different. Wild! I love it!"

"Yeah, different. The only problem is it can't last long."

"You get tired?"

"No, I shoot off fast this way like a stick of dynamite."

He did, smashing harder and harder until the whole world evaporated in a huge cloud of fire and smoke that vaporized everything within sight or hearing. He almost collapsed on the floor before they staggered back to the bed and fell on it still exhausted.

They lay there until their breath stopped coming in huge gasps and the panting phase slowed and stopped.

"Are you hungry?" Willa asked with a sly grin.

He dressed and went to the hotel dining room and came back with two fried chicken dinners and a small bottle of wine. They ate and then he changed clothes, putting on jeans and a heavy shirt and his leather vest for riding.

"I have an appointment," he said. "Man I have to go see."

Willa sat on the bed and shook her breasts at him. "Wouldn't you rather stay here and see if you could make a clean breast of these?"

Morgan laughed. "True, I'd like to try, but maybe next time. I really do have to leave."

She began dressing, then kissed him hard on the mouth.

"I want to see you again, soon. Tonight?"

"Busy tonight, maybe in a couple of days. I'm here on business and if I don't do it I can't afford to buy you dinner."

She kissed him again, then finished dressing. At last she checked the hall and when it was clear, slipped out of his room and went down to hers, 211, the lucky room number.

Morgan strapped on his gunbelt and the Colt, then headed for the livery and his bay. An Indian with a college degree? This he had to see to believe.

Chapter Six

Morgan had a general direction, north. He knew the Sioux would camp along one of the tributaries that ran into the Platte, which narrowed his search since there weren't that many small rivers flowing in Nebraska.

He had checked the best railroad maps but most of them extended less than twenty miles on each side of the tracks. It was all they needed to find the Land Grants from the government for building the road.

He just hoped the band of Sioux he was looking for were not all the way up to the headwaters of the South Loop River which was at least thirty miles north. His report said Schoolboy White Eagle lived with a band "close to North Platte," whatever that meant. He might get lucky.

Five miles north he chanced on a small stream not on the map. It came down from the north but angled off to the east. Any stream in a storm. From what he knew of the Sioux, he realized that these were not reservation Indians. Nor were they town Indians.

He had no chance of riding up to the camp and asking about a man called Schoolboy White Eagle. He would have to sneak into their camp after dark. It was not an exciting possibility.

Morgan rode for another hour and figured he was about thirteen or fourteen miles from North Platte. He came to a small bluff over the stream which was growing smaller and smaller each mile. Morgan tied his bay in the brush along the water and crawled up the bluff which was not over fifty feet off the surface of the plains.

In Nebraska that's nearly a mountain. He could see ten miles ahead through a light afternoon haze. Less than a mile ahead, the haze deepened and he could sniff the light tang of wood smoke. It had to be an Indian camp.

Morgan rode forward, being careful to stay in the cover of the brush along the creek.

Any band that camped on a water flow this small would have to be few in number. A horse alone needed twenty gallons of water a day. Morgan took his time, checked the area carefully for hunters, and moved ahead cautiously.

He wouldn't be able to go into the camp until he made sure it was the right one, and then not until after dark. Before then he had to make sure this was the *right* camp, and then spot which tipi was Schoolboy White Eagle's. Morgan prayed that this was the band Schoolboy rode with. The report said the literate Indian had an eagle painted on the top of his tipi.

An hour before sunset, Morgan tied his horse in some fresh grass inside the brush and worked his way forward on foot. Now he lay near a bend in the small stream. It was larger here in volume than below. Various springs fed it, and here and there it bled out into a narrow valley watering it deeply.

Across the water and 100 yards upstream, he saw fifteen tipis. They were the usual plains Indian tipi of buffalo hide and ten to twelve upright poles. He checked the six tipis closest but saw no eagle.

With great caution, he worked ahead another 25 yards to view one side of three more tipis, and then he saw it. A screaming eagle with extended claws ready to strike had been painted on the topside of the tipi. The shelter sat nearly in the center of the dwellings.

Nothing was easy on this job.

He saw women and children playing around the tipis. Three small girls ran to the stream and pulled off their simple breechclouts and splashed in the shallow water. Among the tipis, he saw several men. One walked a pony through the camp toward the far end where the horses must be kept.

For a moment he saw a man come out of the eagle tent. A warrior stood there, with no shirt, but wearing white man's pants. He called to someone, laughed and went back inside. That must be Schoolboy.

Morgan had not thought to bring along any food in his saddlebags. He drank from the stream and waited. Darkness came slowly. When it was fully settled in, Morgan worked silently forward along the stream, picked a rocky place and walked across. The water was only three or four inches deep there.

On the far side he paused in the brush and watched the camp for five minutes before he moved. No one walked around outside. He had not seen any lookouts or guards. He heard people talking, a gush of laughter, then quiet.

Slowly Morgan moved up to the back of the first

tipi. His nerves were raw from trying to sense any sound, see any movement. He edged around this conical shelter and walked upright to the next one. There he paused, squatted, his Colt out and ready. Nothing moved.

He walked to the eagle tipi and paused again. Another laugh. Ahead, a warrior came out of the flap of his tipi and a pale yellow light, perhaps from the fire, splashed across the ground, then was gone. The man walked away from the stream, relieved himself and went back in his dwelling.

Morgan moved toward the flap on the eagle tipi. He paused just a moment, then lifted the flap and rushed inside in one motion, the weapon up.

The front of the tipi was lighted by a small blazing fire. A woman bent over it cooking. At the side a kerosene lamp burned and beside it, sitting in a folding chair beside a small table, was Schoolboy White Eagle.

The educated Indian looked up.

"Schoolboy, I come in peace," Morgan said.

The woman hissed and raised a knife, but a soft word from Schoolboy stopped her.

"Come in, welcome to my home. Whoever you are, you are a brave man to sneak up on a Sioux camp."

Morgan slid the Colt into leather. "My name is Morgan and I come to talk, nothing more. Agreed?"

"I am not a savage, Mr. Morgan. Please come, sit down, I even have a second chair. Small Feet, my woman, does not believe in the white eye's chair." He unfolded a second one and put it beside the table.

Morgan sat down and grinned. "Just like Boston," he said.

"I don't know Boston. I went to school in Chicago. I should have a beer for you. The fact of the matter is that I drank the last of my supply a week ago. I need to go into North Platte for some of the necessities of life that my brother Sioux do not seem to need."

"Business, Schoolboy. Since you go to North Platte, you must have heard about the robbery of railroad patent deeds to land that took place about six months ago."

"Indeed I have, Mr. Morgan. A curious affair since the deeds would need to be signed over by the rail officials to be negotiable."

Morgan grinned. "Damn, you talk English better than I do. I congratulate you on your education."

"A chance happening. Not really my doing at all. You probably know the story. But to business. I have heard of the robbery and the murder. Beyond that, I know little. There was a town Indian, Young Fox, who had been in North Platte for over a year. He was from our band and chose to go to the white eye village.

"About that time he disappeared. I tried to find him in North Platte, but nobody had seen him there. There's a chance he was involved somehow with the robbery. Young fox was not a Christian, he had little understanding of right and wrong. He could be talked into doing anything."

Morgan thought it over. "You remember nothing else happening here? No one came into your camp? No white eyes came and asked you to help them in exchange for some land?"

White Eagle took out makings and rolled a cigarette. Morgan grinned as he watched him.

"First Indian I ever saw roll a smoke," Morgan said.

White Eagle lit the twist and smiled. "I am the first Indian to do many things." His face saddened. "You spoke of land. It is a raging need of my people. The reservations will be the poorest land the government can find. We need a section for each Sioux living in my village. I would die for land for my people. But, we are not 'citizens,' we cannot file homesteads, we cannot buy land." He shook his head.

"Even if you found the grant deeds, they would be worthless to you."

"I know, that troubles me as well. How can I help my people when the laws I learned prevent us from owning land?"

They talked for more than an hour. Morgan was amazed at what this educated Indian knew, how quick and smart he was. If anyone could help the Sioux, Schoolboy White Eagle was the man.

His woman brought food and they ate. It was rabbit stew with generous amounts of potatoes, carrots and some other vegetables. It was delicious. Also on hand were some small biscuits.

"How in the world. . . ." Morgan began.

Schoolboy laughed. "I missed the biscuits, so I built a reflector oven from an old five gallon metal can, set it close to the fire built against a back log, and it works well. I mix and bake the biscuits myself—but don't tell the other warriors."

Morgan chuckled. "Our secret."

An hour later, Schoolboy took Morgan through the camp and to his horse.

"No sentries, no scouts, guards?" Morgan asked.

"We are not at war. We are getting ready for the next hunt in two or three weeks. There is a lot of work to do."

"If you hear of anything about the patent deeds or those two white men, send me a message to the hotel."

"I'll do it. The next time I come to town I'll find you and I'll buy you that beer I owe you. One of the bartenders is my friend."

Morgan waved, turned the bay and rode off south, out of the brush, angling for the distant sound of a train whistle on the Union Pacific tracks nearly fifteen miles to the south.

Much later that night, Schoolboy White Eagle tied his horse to a post in the alley in back of the Purple Garter Saloon in North Platte. He moved past two closed up tent buildings and to the next frame store that pushed deeper into the alley. He was about to knock on the back door when a man with a gun jumped out of the shadows.

"Okay, Schoolboy, I thought that was you. It's way past time that you and me have a long talk."

Schoolboy raised his hands when he saw the moonlight glint off the six-gun.

"I'm sorry, sir, you have the advantage of me."

"Don't use your dandified manners, Schoolboy. I'm Alexis Savage, with the Pinkertons. You know me, we talked two, three times before. You and me gonna have a good long talk." ·

"I wish I could, Mr. Savage, but I don't have a lot of time just now."

"Make time," Savage snarled. He stepped closer and the six-gun slammed down across the side of Schoolboy's head, driving him to the ground. Blood oozed from two long gashes. Schoolboy sat on the ground in the dirt of the alley.

"What do you wish to talk about, Mr. Savage?"

"Where are the damned patent deeds? Where is that satchel the courier carried? I know damned well that it came into Injun country the day after it was taken. I think you know. You don't tell me, here, tonight, you're gonna be nothing but another dead redskin by morning."

"Mr. Savage, I told you when we spoke before that I knew nothing then. I have heard nothing since then. Your suppositions may be valid, but I have no way of knowing. None of the men in the camp have mentioned it. They would not consider such a satchel or the white eye papers valuable. Why should they?"

COLT CROSSING • 57

"You must have heard something. Did you see that town Indian, Young Fox, after he left town?"

"No. He was here. He disappeared from here the same afternoon of the robbery. If there is a connection, I do not know of it."

"Quit the damn uppity talk, Injun!" Savage barked.

"I speak the only way I know how."

Savage bent to hit him again with the gun. This time White Eagle was ready. He grabbed the gun hand, pulled Savage forward and threw him into the dirt. The six-gun skidded away into the darkness.

Schoolboy White Eagle leaped up and darted down the alley the other way. Savage found his gun and fired five shots but none of them touched White Eagle. Schoolboy had to wait for an hour before the alley was clear of the curious so he could slip in and get his horse.

Perhaps it would not be a good idea to see the man he had intended to see, after all. There would be another time.

Schoolboy White Eagle slipped in the back door of the saloon where his friend worked, bought six bottles of beer with money from his white eye pants pocket, and opened one of them as he began his long ride back to his Sioux camp fifteen miles to the north.

Chapter Seven

It was nearly nine A.M. before Morgan struggled out of his bed at the Nebraskan hotel. Nobody had tried to kill him last night, at least. He pondered about Schoolboy White Eagle. He was the strangest Indian Morgan had ever met—he was more intelligent, smarter and better educated than most of the whites in the West. Which would make his difficult course in life even harder.

Morgan dressed, splashed cold water in his face to try to wake up, and walked over to Marleen's for breakfast.

"You slept late," Marleen said as she poured an oversized cup of coffee for him. It was one of her special large mugs. Today she wore a white blouse and blue skirt and was as pretty as a lady bug on a bluebell.

"Had some catching up to do."

The breakfast crowd was gone. He was the only

one in the little cafe. After she fixed his breakfast she sat in the chair at the end of the counter and worked on a cup of coffee, watching him eat.

"Do you travel?" he said suddenly.

She looked him directly in the eye showing a curious smile.

"I was thinking if you did, I'd put you in my suitcase and take you along to fix breakfast for me every morning for the rest of my life."

"It's an idea, but remember, you haven't tried my supper yet. Don't make any silly offers until you try my supper."

"By then it may be too late."

Marleen laughed. "Sure, I get offers to travel all over the West every ten minutes. Hey, this is a railroad town."

Morgan watched her as he ate. He liked the way she had her dark hair cut short around her face and in back. No long hair to get in the way of her cooking. She was taller than most women and he saw a quality there, a strength, an iron will. Marleen was not the kind of woman you bedded and walked away from.

Before she slept with a man they both would know that it was a long time commitment. He mentally put her in a special category he kept for such untouchable women. At least she could still be a friend.

"Remember when the railroad courier was kidnapped and then murdered?"

She looked up and nodded. "Yes, Mr. Gorman. He ate in here a couple of times when he stayed over. He was a good man."

"Do you know anything about what happened that day? Who might have been involved?"

Her forehead wrinkled a moment as she thought about it. "No," not enough to get anyone in trouble. I hear bits and pieces of talk sometimes in here, but it was nothing."

"Marleen, I'm in town to try to find those documents. They are extremely valuable. They are deeds to 400 sections of Nebraska land."

Her brows went up. "So much? Goodness, that is a lot. That's a piece of land twenty miles long and twenty miles wide!"

She went to the kitchen a moment, then came back wiping her hands.

"I did hear something once, and it may not be important. He's a good customer . . . I don't know."

"Nobody will be hurt if he had nothing to do with the robbery and murder. It was a brutal killing."

"His hand . . . all right. I heard something that at the time made me think that Lame Charlie might know more than he should about the whole thing. Just a word here and there. I'm not sure." She frowned. "Oh, dear. I don't think I should have told you."

"You did the right thing. Don't worry. Now, how do you fix these potatoes? They're wonderful."

"Old family secret," she said quickly, then grinned. "No, just boil them, let them cool and then fry them with a touch of butter to get a little golden crisp on the outside. Easy."

"When you know how." He slid off the chair, paid his tab and smiled at her on the way out. A great way to start the day.

"Press day," Lame Charlie said when Morgan stepped into the rail car.

"We need to talk."

"Talk, but don't get in my way. I have to print off three hundred copies before tomorrow morning. Six pages this issue!"

"Congratulations."

"Yeah, but that's twelve hundred times I have to

pull that press lever. Most people don't know what a hell of a lot of work it is putting out a newspaper. Would you swing that press lever for me? Be a big help. I ain't got one of them fancy automatic presses yet."

"A sheet at a time?"

"One side of a sheet at a time. Do a hundred on one side, then turn them over when they get dry and print the other side. Turns into work."

"Penny a copy?"

"When I can sell them. Mostly I give them away so the advertisers will keep taking ads."

Morgan pushed the big lever over bringing the pressure plate down over the page form where Lame Charlie had just spread a sheet of newsprint. The pressure printed the page and he swung the lever back lifting the heavy plate up and Lame Charlie took out the page.

"Yep, the page looks good. I might hire you."

"Charlie, you're holding out on me. You know a lot more about the patent deed robbery than you told me. I want you to tell me the rest of it right now."

Lame Charlie looked up quickly. His hand shook just a moment as he put a new sheet of paper over the page form. He pushed the lever that time himself.

"Told you what I knew yesterday when you were here."

"You told me enough to get rid of me. I think you're in this right up to your eyebrows, Charlie. You better get out while you can."

"I don't know what you're talking about."

"You better, Charlie. These people are not soft hearted. They'll throw you into the wolf pit as soon as talk to you. Look what happened to the courier. This is big time, a big money robbery, and the men behind it won't hesitate to blow your brains out. Think it over."

"Nothing to think about. I have a newspaper to get out."

"Mr. Quenton Johnson will be in town in two days. I don't want to have to give him a bad report about you. He'll throw your private car here off the siding so fast all of your type cases will be pied. Think about it, Charlie."

Morgan threw the big lever one more time then checked the page when Charlie took it off.

"Saw a printer who had one hand mangled in a press like this. Broke damn near every bone in his hand." Morgan turned and walked away without another word.

When he left the rail car, Lee went to the first building up from the tracks and slipped around the corner. He stopped and eased back to the edge of the building, squatted low and looked back at the rail car so he couldn't be seen.

Nothing happened for five minutes. Then Lame Charlie came out of the box car. He had his printer's apron off and his cane. He slammed the door on the box car, locked it and limped down the wooden steps and along the tracks to the next street.

Morgan followed him as closely as he could without being seen. Lame Charlie went up the street, turned in the alley and limped halfway down, then walked through the back door of a frame building.

The doorway was the second frame building from the corner. Morgan went to the street and checked the second frame structure. It was the one "office" building in North Platte. Signs boasted four firms inside, two on the ground floor, a lawyer and a branch of the U.S. district land office. On the second floor were the offices of a surveyor and an accountant.

None seemed a likely stop for Lame Charlie. He could have slipped through the hallway and out the front door. Morgan looked up and down the street but didn't see the tall, thin, lame man.

Damn! This was getting complicated. Right now he yearned for a horse chase, a shootout and a good clean decision—either yes or no. Finish the job and get on with a new one. That wasn't going to happen on this assignment. Christ, how did he get mixed up in a job like this? Told the damn boss he was no detective. Kick ass was what he did best, but now there were no asses to kick.

Lee Morgan swore to himself as he walked across the street and into the best looking of the three bars. This one was a real frame building with a wooden floor.

Inside he got a beer at the bar and sat at a table next to the wall and watched the people. It wasn't noon yet and the drinkers were sparse. Two of the saloon's soiled doves wandered down from up-stairs. A frazzled blonde in her thirties had a shot of whiskey for breakfast and headed toward the back door.

The second one was younger, looked to be no more than sixteen. The barkeep poured her a glass of milk from a gallon jug he took from the ice box. The young girl took it and went back up the steps probably to her crib. Work time for the girls didn't start until after noon.

Morgan shook his head. His problems didn't seem so great after all. All he had to deal with was a satchel full of missing patent deeds that would be worth a hundred million dollars if somebody could hold on to them for fifty years. He had no clues, no leads, no tracks, no trail, no suspects.

He tipped the beer bottle. Every town had a different tasting beer in the West. Usually a town of any size had its own brewery and the beer had a taste that reflected the quality of the ground water. Now with the railroad, some of the big breweries from the East would probably be sending their products West.

Morgan looked up. The barman stood beside his table. He handed Morgan a folded piece of paper torn from a writing tablet. He opened it and read:

"Morgan, see me now in the storeroom. I might have something to help you. Kasper Gorman was a good friend of mine." It was signed only with the letter "H."

When Morgan asked the apron where the storeroom was and waved the note, the man indicated the second door down the hallway to the alley.

In front of the door, Morgan loosened the Colt in his leather, then opened the door slowly and looked inside. It was filled with boxes, a rack of bottles not being used and a sawhorse with a saddle over it. Sitting on a box smoking a thin cigar was the frazzled blonde he had seen earlier.

She looked up. "Mr. Morgan?"

"Yes." He glanced around quickly. There was no one else in the small room, no place for anyone to hide and no windows.

"I'm Holly. I knew Kasper Gorman and I want to kill the men who tortured and murdered him."

"You know who they are?"

"I might, I'm not sure. Kasper was more than a customer. He was a good friend. We talked about getting married." She glared at him for a minute. "Yeah, some man wanted me enough to forget all this and take me away. Probably my last damn chance." She blinked and wiped moisture away from her cheeks and eyes. "Yeah, I want those bastards. Two of them at least. Will you help me?"

"Why did you pick me?"

"You're in town for the Union Pacific trying to find the lost patent deeds. I know all about them.

If I help you find the right men, can I have the bastards?"

"To kill?"

"Sounds like a good idea. They have it coming. All done with a little personal justice thrown in for good measure."

"Been known to indulge myself that way a few times. If I capture them alive, you get them. Now, what do you know, Holly?"

"Kasper was afraid something might happen to him. He said he was too well known, had been making the deliveries too long. This was to be his last trip."

"Did he plan to steal the goods with some other men? Don't get mad, I have to ask."

"No. Kasper was as honest as a preacher. He never even thought of doing anything like that. He was a sweet, gentle man. They wouldn't let him carry a gun at first. When they made him carry one he had to learn how to shoot it."

"Who here in town is involved in the robbery?"

"Men talk when they're with me. You know, brag, tell things they never would if they weren't trying to impress a girl. Some of them need the kick to get it up. Anyway, I hear lots of things I shouldn't. Once I got beat up because I reminded a guy what he said. He threatened to kill me.

"Now I just listen, am impressed, tell them how great they are, and then forget what they said. Except Sly Fox."

"The town Indian?"

"Yes. I guess none of the other girls in town would take him on. I was always looking for something new. So he was a Sioux, he was no different from a white man. But usually he was drunk and that slowed him down and he liked to talk. Proud of his English. Kept telling me about this big important deal he had coming up.

"Then one night he was real drunk. He wanted to stay with me, but he couldn't even get it hard. So we talked. He told me about it. Said he'd be the richest Indian in the Plains. Said he was working with two white eyes."

"Names, did he mention anybody's name?"

"Said he was working with Shorty Wilberton. I've done him a time or two. Shorty's been around town half a year before the robbery. Then the day of the robbery Shorty vanished. Nobody in town ever saw him again."

"Young Fox tell you the plan?"

"Young Fox was no Schoolboy White Eagle. He was a little slow, and his English wasn't perfect. But he told me they would stop the train. He got to play trainman in the overalls and train cap. Oh, Young Fox had his hair cut short while he was in town so he fit in better. He said then they'd take the goods off the train."

She looked up and tears wet her cheeks again. "I had no idea they were going after the patent deeds and Kasper. If I'd known that I would have stabbed Sly Fox through the heart right there!"

She took several big breaths, and wiped her eyes and went on.

"Anyway, He said they would get the goods and take off into Indian country where he could protect his white partner from any white eyes who might follow them."

She looked away. "He said something about hiding the stolen goods in Indian country until it was safe to bring them out. Said he'd be the richest damn Indian in the world."

"Who was his partner, did he say?"

She thought for a minute. "Not for sure. One night he said he was going to quit the whole thing if he had to do the hard work anymore. Young Fox was against work of any kind. He'd rather drink and fuck and lay around. Then one night he told me he had been working the big press lever down at the newspaper. Said he was stiff and sore and damn tired of doing it every week. Do you suppose . . . Could it be he was working on the robbery scheme with Lame Charlie Bard?"

Chapter Eight

Morgan left the dance hall girl and headed for the Sheriff's office. In this county it was in a framed tent halfway down Main Street next to the hardware tent. There was no jail. The county hadn't been around long enough yet to get its property taxation system into operation.

The office consisted of a desk, a pair of chairs, two lamps and a strong gun rack with a lock on it. The county could afford to pay only for one deputy.

Sheriff Emery Lewis, leaned back in the chair and nodded.

"Figured it was you. About time you come to get the official report about that killing. Been hearing around town that you're here to snoop for the railroad big bosses. I dug out my report to the grand jury. We got a great little crime here but absolutely no suspects."

"And a body without one hand," Morgan said after he had introduced himself. "Anything developed in that case after six months?"

"Nary a thing. The Union Pacific gents are pestering me with letters and investigators every other day. I can't find evidence that ain't there. They so much as said I was right when they pulled the Pinkertons off it. Case like this got so many twists and turns and dead ends that it just can't be solved."

"Why, you figure?"

The sheriff hitched up his pants over an expanding belly, settled his six-gun in the holster and stared out the flap of the front door at the street.

"Way I figure it is there was a falling out of thieves, or train robbers in this case. Two of them, right? So could have been that they buried them fancy papers and then one killed the other one so he could have it all. Spelled G-R-E-E-D."

"But none of the goods have shown up. Nobody has ever tried to ransom the papers. Why the long wait?"

"That is a problem. So maybe it wasn't greed. In that case I come up with this one. The two of them hid the goods in a safe place, then one sneaks back and takes that damned satchel and hides it in a different place. Then the one skunk shoots down the one who re-hid the goods cause he wants it all. Only now nobody alive knows where the goods is, especially the one who killed his partner. So the killer hunts it, but he ain't about to find it."

"Could be. If so I'm not going to make a whole lot of money on this job."

"Yeah, get a new job. Your name Morgan? Seemed like I had a wanted poster on a Morgan."

"Common name, sheriff. I had a lot of trouble with a gent using the same name as mine a while back. He was out in Wyoming or Utah, or somewhere out there. There was some Wanteds on him. Maybe they tracked down the polecat by now.''

"This one had a picture," the sheriff said. "Well, if it's here, I'll find it come a week of Sundays." The lawman looked up. "You got any theories about who the robber/killers are?"

"Yep. Figure they come from right here in town. Also figure that one of them was Shorty Wilberton, remember him? Little guy who used to cadge drinks all over town, got himself shot up once or twice."

"Shorty? Why him?"

"He came up missing the day of the robbery. Nobody ever seen nor heard of him since. He might have been the one who got himself murdered right out of a fortune."

"But they was two of them. Who else?"

"If I knew, I'd have a body for you to hold on to while I went out and found the satchel."

"Figures."

"I have some questions about some of the local folks. How well do you know the banker?"

"Ivan? Only man in town with money. Good, decent man. Not a chance there that he's involved in this."

"What about the livery stable man? Seemed to me I've seen his face before on the hoot owl trail."

"Old man Hightower? You got to be joking. He's in hog heaven running his livery. Fact is, the town didn't have a livery operation until Ivan loaned Hightower all the cash he needed to start the place. Hightower has it almost paid back already. Don't try to horsetrade with Old Hightower, he'll clean out your wagon box every time."

"Guess I'm shinnying up the wrong pole. Talked with the young newspaper man, what's his name, Charlie?"

"Everybody calls him Lame Charlie. He doesn't seem to mind. Knee got busted up by a runaway carriage when he was a boy. Don't know a lot about Charlie. Puts out a nice little newspaper. Lot of work for one man. Solid citizen around here."

"He gave me all the clippings he had printed in the paper about the robbery." Morgan stood and looked at a wanted poster pinned to the side of the tent. A $500 reward. That would attract a lot of bounty hunters. "Thanks for the talk. I better start earning my wages. Mr. Johnson himself is coming to town in a day or two."

"Quenton Johnson himself is doing us the honor of a visit? I better deputize a few more men. Certain of the farmers don't like the way his railroad grants are gobbling up all the best land. Best land for farm homesteading is already gone, they say."

Morgan nodded and stepped to the door. "Thanks, Sheriff, I'll be around." Morgan went into the street and heard a clock strike twelve in one of the stores. He wasn't ready to eat again.

"Ho! You there!" A voice called from behind. Morgan kept walking ahead.

"Ho! You with the red diamonds on your hat band."

This time Morgan figured the man was talking to him. He let his right hand swing easily at his side near the Colt and turned around slowly.

Thirty feet away on the boardwalk stood the man who had killed the gambler in the saloon. His name was Wild Bill Nelson. He'd been half blind drunk that night, but he was sober now, neatly dressed and his gun hand wavered near his iron.

"You screeching at me?" Morgan bellowed.

Wild Bill laughed and walked forward until he was twenty feet from Morgan and no one was between them.

"We ain't met, stranger, but I don't like the low way you carry your piece. Not crazy about the way you tie down your leather either, like you can use that hogleg."

"That what's stuck in your gizzard, Nelson?"

"You know my name."

"Saw you kill a man, break his back over a saloon bar couple of nights back. You were roaring drunk."

"Happened. He shot me. You got a reason for packing that Colt so low?"

"You should know." Morgan tensed, saw the big man's hand quiver over his iron.

"Easy way we can find out if you can use that iron," Wild Bill said.

People on the boardwalk paused, then stepped off into the street. Suddenly there was no one in back of either man and one shop owner nearby came out and closed wooden shutters over two glass windows in the front of his store. There was a long pause as they stared at each other.

"We try to find out who is faster with the iron and one of us is dead," Morgan said evenly.

Wild Bill studied him a moment. "What the hell's your name?"

"Lee Morgan."

Wild Bill wrinkled his brow. "You from out Idaho way?"

"Could be."

Wild Bill grinned. "You ever hear of William Buckskin Frank Leslie and the Spade Bit ranch?"

"Heard of it," Morgan admitted.

"Heard of it, hell, you were raised on it. You're whelp of Buckskin Frank Leslie. I'll be damned!"

The tension went out of the meeting. People relaxed, moved back on the boardwalk and went about their business. Someone opened the shutters on the store.

Morgan and Wild Bill walked up to each other and stared.

"I rode with your pap when you was just a

chigger. He talked about you half the time."

"I've heard of your name in the last two or three years," Morgan said. "You've been moving about a bit."

"Whichever way the wind blows, and the cash grows. Hiring out to get a job done."

Wild Bill looked at the tied down holster again. "Could be you're in the same line of work?"

"Could be. I had a fine teacher."

"Fine? Buckskin Frank Leslie was the best. You as fast as him?"

"Don't guess. Glad I never had to draw against him. But I learned good."

"You got time for a beer, Morgan?"

"I can cut out a few minutes. We can talk about the Spade Bit. You been up there lately?"

They went down the boardwalk to the Golden Nugget Saloon and found a table. They ordered three beers each and set the bottles side by side.

"Never forget the first day I saw you pap. He had signed on as security chief for a Cattleman's Association out in Montana, and six men rode into town just after he arrived. The leader, a gent called Hopping Mad Harry, snarled out a challenge to Frank to come out and face the music.

"Frank was in a poker game and had just drawn to a full house and there was twenty dollars in the pot. He made everybody put down his hand and come outside with him. He told the apron to watch the cards.

"Outside he saw the six men. They had been rustling as many steers as they could drive from the local ranchers during the past few months. Now they were upset with your pap for saying he was going to stop them.

"Old Frank didn't say two words. Three of the men were still on their horses. Frank pulled his Colt and nailed two of them on the ground right in the heart with his first two shots, then dove behind a water trough and shot another one off his horse. Three tried to run but he shot the fourth one out of leather and would have had a fifth but his last round misfired.

"Two got away and the town had a grand funeral and the Cattleman's Association paid your pap the five hundred dollars. He'd spent about two minutes total on the job. Back in the saloon your pap won the pot with his full house and the twenty dollar pot. He talked more about winning that pot than he did gunning down those four men when it was six to one against him."

They talked for an hour. Then the three beers were gone and Morgan pushed back from the table.

"Who you working for here?" Morgan asked.

"Big outfit. Nobody's supposed to know but I'm on the Union Pacific payroll. My job is to keep the town halfway respectable and watch for anyone stealing railroad property or supplies."

Morgan grinned. "Same outfit I signed on with. I'm supposed to find those railroad papers robbed off the train six months ago. You know anything about that?"

"Not a damn thing. Thought the Pinks were working on that."

"Johnson fired them. Now it's up to me."

"If I hear anything, it's yours."

They stood and shook hands. "We'll have to talk about the Spade Bit again. Reminds me of home."

When Morgan left, Wild Bill went up to the bar looking for something else to drink.

By four o'clock that afternoon, Morgan had tramped the town, talked to a dozen people, but nobody could remember anything helpful about that fateful day six months ago when the train was robbed.

He gave up for the day and stepped into the

quiet of the little cafe. Marleen came out of the
back room.

"You missed your noon feeding time," she said.
"Unless you ate somewhere else."

"I missed it. What's for supper?"

She brought him a pound of T-bone steak,
mashed potatoes and brown gravy, three
vegetables, fresh baked bread rolls, jam, coffee,
and fresh cinnamon applesauce for desert.

Marleen sat beside him in a chair and sipped a
cup of hot tea. "You hear the big news?"

He looked up from the supper. "News?"

"Yes, our beloved U.S. Senator from Nebraska,
Stanwick Perridale, is arriving tomorrow for an
inspection tour of the Union Pacific, the stock
yards, and the district point."

"Why?"

"He didn't tell me," Marleen said and laughed.
"He's on the Senate Transportation Committee,
the big one pushing the transcontinental railroad.
It's a trip to report to the committee how things
are moving along."

Morgan grunted. "I'll have to have a talk with
the Senator, straighten him out."

Marleen looked up quickly, then saw he was
joking.

It was the best meal Morgan had eaten in a
week.

Chapter Nine

Everyone in town was soon talking about the senator coming. Word had arrived in a telegram to the sheriff asking him to have two men at the station to meet the senator and to act as his guides and extra bodyguards during his stay.

Sheriff Lewis picked out two young men who knew how to use their guns, pinned deputy sheriff badges on them and hired them at two dollars a day for as long as the Senator was in town.

Morgan heard people around town talking about the Senator like he was a minor god. They said he was responsible for the town's very existence. If it hadn't been for the railroad there would be no town of North Platte.

The senator was due in on the 6:04 train westbound. Morgan wandered down to the station with half of the rest of the town. There were dance hall girls, cowboys, merchants and housewives all standing around in the soft late afternoon, waiting for the train.

Morgan saw Lame Charlie limp up with his pad of paper and two pencils in his pocket. He was sure the newsman would be there. The Senator would be the lead story in the next issue of the *Pioneer On Wheels*.

The man from the Spade Bit ranch in Idaho watched Lame Charlie as he talked with the mayor and then the sheriff, probably getting quotes from them about the ilustrious senator. Morgan had never heard of him before. Since Nebraska became a state in 1867 he had been in the senate only a short time. Lee had no idea who the second senator from Nebraska was.

A shout went up down the line and someone said he had heard a train whistle. Some men put their ears on the steel rail and stood up shouting that the 6:04 was on the way.

It hissed and roared and ground up to the small wooden station and the train high platform ten minutes later. The first man off the train's one passenger car was the senator.

Morgan was not impressed by his appearance. He looked about 55, maybe a year or two more. White hair and a small neatly trimmed white moustache made him look like an Omaha furniture store dealer, which is what he had been until a year ago.

The senator was five-ten, heavy at about 190 pounds, and had a red face that looked like he was constantly blushing. He'd tried everything to get rid of it but nothing worked. He had on a Western hat and smoked a long brown cigar when he walked off the train with both hands high in the air in greeting.

There was no band in town to play, but the locals whooped it up into a minor celebration, cheering the senator, rushing up to ask for his autograph, and telling him what a wonderful man he was. He went to the biggest meeting place in town, the Ticor Saloon and gambling house, for his welcome speech. It soon was filled to over-flowing even though the senator had ordered all liquor sales stopped during his short talk.

Morgan did not venture inside. He'd heard one senator talk once, three or four years ago. That had been his fill of politicians for life. He leaned back a chair in front of the hardware store and tried to sort out what he had on the case. It wasn't a hell of a lot.

The newsman might be involved. The lady of the evening said it was just possible. Was she too eager to get revenge for her man who got himself killed being a courier for the railroad? The way his luck was running it was not only possible, but likely.

So he was back to Schoolboy White Eagle. The man had been sincere. If the two whites had come into the Indian community the day of or the day after the robbery, he would find out.

Then the town Indian, Lame Fox. He as much as told Holly that he was part of the plan. That he would wear the railroad clothes and flag down the train. Now Lame Fox was missing as well. If he was part of it and took his white partner into Indian country like he said he would, what happened next?

That also left out the whereabouts of Shorty Wilberton. There had been two robbers at the train, not three. But he had three potential suspects. Shorty could have simply forked his horse and moved on down the line. Or he could have bought a one way ticket to Denver.

If Lame Charlie had been one of the robbers wouldn't somebody have seen his limp? It was a signature that the stiff knee could not disguise. Evidently, Lame Charlie had not been on the train—too easy to spot. But that still left Shorty. Lame Charlie could have met them to the north.

Morgan closed his eyes, pulled down his hat to cover them and relaxed. Tomorrow would be another day. Maybe he'd have a great idea tonight to solve the case. The sun came down warm, but not too hot today, and Morgan relaxed a little more. He snoozed, woke with the jangle of harness in front of him and then when the rig had passed had a short nap.

A half hour after the crowd had surged into the saloon to hear the senator, they came spewing out. Evidently the man from Washington D.C. had said all the right things. The people were smiling and talking about "their" senator.

Five minutes later, Morgan considered trying out one of the saloons and passing the time with some nickel and dime poker, when Sheriff Lewis stopped in front of his chair.

"Figured that I'd find you working," the Sheriff said. "Don't know why, but the Senator asked me to find you. He wants to talk to you in about fifteen minutes in his hotel suite on the second floor of the Nebraskan Hotel."

"Don't say."

"Just did." The sheriff sat down in the chair next to Morgan's and tipped it back. "I remember that little man when he ran his furniture store in Omaha. I used to live back there. He was close with a dollar. Peers he's changed considerable. 'Cept now it's public money he's working with. From what I've seen, he spends public money like it was water in a flood."

They sat there in silence for a few minutes. "Never did like the looks of that little man, still don't," the elected sheriff of Lincoln county Nebraska said. "Course now he's a big assed United States Senator."

Morgan eased back in his chair. "Yeah, he's a

big man now. Over a few years I learned one thing. No matter how big a man gets, he still pisses yellow just like the rest of us common folks."

Sheriff Lewis slapped his thigh and laughed. Morgan dropped the front legs of the chair to the boardwalk, stood and moved toward the hotel. Wouldn't do to keep the U.S. Senator waiting. What was his name again? Yeah, Senator Stanwick Perridale. Second floor.

As soon as he came to the second story, a man held up his hand.

"Sir, do you have business here?"

"Yes, I live on this floor and I have an appointment with Senator Perridale. That good enough?"

"Yes sir." The man with a revolver in a holster at his side stepped back. "Third door down on the right, number 220."

"How long you been out of the army?"

"Two months, sir."

"Thought so," Morgan said and moved down the hall. At the door of room 220, stood another guard. He had his revolver in his hand poised down.

"I'll have to ask you to leave your weapon with me, sir," the copy of the first young man said.

"Just don't drop it," Morgan said. He handed the Colt over and the man knocked on the door. It came open from the inside. The third guard glanced at Morgan. Saw the empty holster.

"Sir, do you have any other weapons?"

"Just a pocket knife and it's not exactly deadly."

"Let him in, you boys are causing me all sorts of trouble." The sound came from the Senator himself who stood near the window looking down on the main street.

"These new rail towns develop slowly, don't they? Figured there would be dozens of frame buildings here by now." The man came forward and held out his hand. "Perridale is the name, you must be Lee Morgan."

"That's right, senator. What can I do for you?"

"Just wanted to say howdy, take you by the hand and maybe get another vote when I run again." He watched Morgan for a moment without speaking.

"Then I had another reason. I talked with Quenton Johnson in Omaha before we left. He's interested in hearing from you. No report yet on your work here. Asked me to give you the message. He says you should put your report in an envelope, seal it, put down the day and the time of day on the outside and address it to him simply at Omaha. He said give it to the conductor or brakeman on any train and he'll have it just a few hours later."

"Thanks. Hear you're here on an inspection trip for your transportation committee."

Senator Perridale smiled. "Ostensibly, that's my mission. Of course there are always other purposes as well, like making sure I know how many constituents feel about the issues."

"Sounds good. Senator, do you know what my job is here for the railroad?"

"No, not at all. Probably none of my business. But I do hear that you are a highly paid, and somewhat touchy individual to work with. Am I right?"

"I hope the first part is right. The 'touchy' description depends on whether I'm being treated fairly and know all the facts about a case so I can decide for myself. Does that make sense?"

"Does to me." The senator turned. "I'll be here for two days, if you have anything you want me to report to Quenton, I'll be going back that way when I leave."

It was a dismissal. Morgan was just as glad. He felt a slow dislike for the senator growing as they had spoken. He went to the door and turned to look at the man again. "Oh, Senator Perridale, about that 'touchy' word. If you ever use that description of me again, change that word to damned ornery, I think it fits better."

He pulled the door open, jerked his Colt from the hands of the outside guard and went down to his room and pushed the key in the lock. This time the door stayed still and was locked. He opened it and found no one inside.

He remembered that he had seen a copy of the local paper, and wanted to look it over. He stepped out of his door just in time to see Lame Charlie going into the Senator's room. Interesting, damn unusual. No, maybe it was just for an interview for the newspaper. Maybe.

He got a newspaper from the room clerk below, braved the guards on the stairs and made it back to his room intact. When he opened the paper where he sat on the bed, the two inch wood block letters slammed out at him:

SENATOR VISITS

Morgan read the short story under the headline and saw that it said little more than what was in the headline. No specific reason was given for the visit this close to the rail head, but the senator would be checking on the rail progress.

A question plagued Morgan. How did Lame Charlie know two days ago that the Senator was coming? He had to set the story in type, set up the headline, then print the pages. That wasn't the page he had helped print the other day.

Morgan put the paper down and stretched out on the bed. Tonight as soon as it got dark he was going to pay a visit to the newspaper office. It might show up something interesting, but Morgan had no idea what it could be.

Maybe the lame man did have a hidden hand in the robbery afterall. Damnit! He didn't *want to be a damn detective*.

* * *

Four hours later, the last light went out in the box car on the siding a half block down from main street. Lame Charlie Bard came out, slammed the door and locked it. That wasn't going to stop Morgan.

He had cased the hardware store earlier, found a pair of bolt cutters and ambled out the front door with them as if he'd bought them. Easy. Reminded him of the petty theft period in his life when he was growing up.

He let Lame Charlie limp up to Main and down to the a small little cafe that boasted it had New York fare.

When Charlie was out of sight, Morgan put on a good imitation of Lame Charlie's limp and moved slowly down to the box car. No one was within two blocks of his sight lines. He lifted the multiple levered jaws of the bolt cutters and cut the padlock loop in half with one bite. He spun the steel around, unhooked it from the hasp of the rail door and slid the metal door open.

Inside he closed the door but not enough so someone could lock him in there. Then he lit a match, found a lamp and began his search. It took him over an hour. He put everything back the way it was so Lame Charlie wouldn't know he'd been there.

In back of a file in one of the shelves he found a metal box that had a lock on it, but the lock was not set. Inside he found legal papers, including one that formed a partnership between Lame Charlie Bard and one Stanwick Perridale. It was dated about a year ago and made the now senator a two-thirds owner in the *Pioneer On Wheels* publishing company.

The senator had put up a total of five thousand dollars to buy the press, type, paper and other necessities. Charlie Bard brought to the company his newspapering experience and his work to put out the paper. They split any profits 50-50.

Morgan put the papers back, hesitated with the partnership agreement, then stowed it with the rest. Both parties would have copies.

He made sure everything was in place, then blew out the lamp and put it back where he found it and went over to the door. From his pocket he took his other afternoon requisition item of hardware, a padlock.

It was a near match for the one on the door. Morgan took the old one off, pocketed it and put the new one in its place after rubbing some dirt into the sides to make it look older. He closed the door quietly, fitted the new lock around the hasp, and locked it. He kept the two keys.

Lame Charlie would have a time getting to work in the morning. He might get confused about which key fit which lock. In any case it would give him something to think about.

Senator Perridale owning the newspaper. That was something for Morgan to try to fit into this damn puzzle. Lots of political people owned newspapers. Probably wasn't illegal. But was it anything else? If . . . just maybe . . . if Lame Charlie was in on the robbery, did that mean the Senator was part of the conspiracy, too?

Chapter Ten

After his prowl around the newspaper office, Morgan had a beer in a saloon on his way to his hotel. He wasn't sure if the tie in of the newspaper with the Senator had any bearing on the railroad patent deeds robbery/murder. No reason why it should, but from what Holly said about Young Fox and Lame Charlie. . . .

Morgan gave up and went back to his hotel room in the Nebraskan. At the top of the stairs he found the guard who nodded at him and let him pass, but watched him all the way into his room. The damned Senator seemed afraid of someone or worried about something.

Lee checked the window. The glass was intact and it was locked. He threw the bolt on the door and pushed the chair under the knob, then unbuckled his gun belt and hung it on the iron bed post. He was wondering if he should write down all the names and what he knew about each one. Maybe he could find a pattern.

A knock sounded on his door, sharp, three rapid, insistent tappings. Morgan lifted his Colt out of the leather and went to the door.

"Yes?" Morgan said standing to the wall side of the opening.

"It's Willa," a small voice outside said.

He frowned and moved the chair and moved back the bolt, then pulled the door open. Willa came in quickly and closed the door. She leaned against it and grinned at him.

"It was getting lonely." She indicated a basket on her arm. "I brought you a midnight snack, just in case you were hungry."

"I'm hungry he said. He lifted her and carried her to the bed, pulled open the blouse she wore and massaged her breasts.

"Yes, I like it rough and fast sometimes," she said.

He pushed her long skirt up to her waist and found nothing under it. Morgan growled and opened the fly on his town pants and pulled out his favorite weapon. He was hot and ready. In one quick thrust he drove between her legs and thrust deeply into her, dry skin against dry skin burning for a moment until the natural juices made the going easier.

Morgan took out his frustration of the job on Willa Porterfield, for the moment not caring what she wanted or how she felt. She filled a need for the time being and he was living for the moment. Nothing else mattered.

For a fleeting second he thought of an old outhouse proverb: A stiff prick has no conscience. Right now that was true. He thrust into her hard, savagely, and she moaned and yelped in he hoped pleasure. He wasn't aware how she was reacting, he wanted only to blast his seed, to gain his release. It came quickly and he let her bind him to her for five minutes as he sagged on her beautiful body, mashing it into the mattress.

When she relaxed her arms from where they pinned him to her around his back, he rolled away.

"You were like a wild animal," she said softly. "I loved it, all fire and heat and action, no worry about who you're with or her feelings. It was wonderful! But I don't like it every time like that." She sat up.

"Now, some food to help you get back your strength." She opened the basket on the bed and gave him some fancy crackers already spread with hard cheese. Willa had a small bottle of wine he popped the cork on, and poured into two wine glasses.

"I hear you're working for the railroad. Most everybody does in this town one way or the other. Except me. I'm an outsider."

"You'll get by."

She laughed and it made her big breasts do a little dance. Morgan reached over and petted them.

"Love that," Willa said biting a sweet pickle she took from a small jar. "You can do me about three times a day, all year long, if you want to." She fed him a pickle and some strawberries.

"I got these from the store. They just came in on the train. Aren't they wonderful? I had them dipped in water and then rolled in powdered sugar."

He had two of them.

"So how's your work coming along? Right now seems like lots of people are trying to find those old grant deeds or whatever they are. I hear about it all around town. They say you stirred things up again."

"I'm not finding out much," Morgan said.

Then somewhere a light flickered on. She was

grilling him, trying to find out how much he knew. She wasn't very subtle about it. One of her hands fell to his crotch and she toyed with his genitalia.

"I love this big guy! It always amazes me that he can be so tough and hard one minute, and then later like a big soft worm."

Morgan decided to feed her some false information and see what she did with it. He bent and kissed her, then fed her a strawberry as he fondled her breasts.

"I'm at a dead end on those damn papers. I'm about ready to report that it was an inside job, some trainmen got together, knew the papers were coming. One stopped the train, the engineer said that. Then the trainman kidnapped the courier and killed him and are holding the papers for ransom."

"Oh, that's wonderful, Morgan. How do you figure those things out? I just get lost in there somewhere. I'm not very good at all that mystery stuff. I'm better at this." She humped her crotch upward fast three times and giggled.

"You're damn good at that, Willa. Best I've ever had."

She grinned. "I bet you've poked a lot of girls."

"One or two. Especially when they sit naked on my bed, and come late at night with a midnight supper and with no underwear on."

"I like to make things easy. I'm over being shy and coy. We both know what we want to do, so we should just do it."

"We did."

"That was just once." She pumped his penis trying to get it hard again.

"We have all night."

"Oh, yeah," she said and got both hands into the food again. There were small cookies, more cheese and crackers, and three kinds of candy that looked home made.

"How long you going to be in town?" he asked.

"I don't know. As long as I can have fun I guess. As long as you are, I'd hope. I don't want you to find out about those dumb old railroad papers. I want you to stay forever."

"I'm wrapping it up soon, maybe tomorrow. I've got one good lead I want to check out. The papers may be right here in town!"

He eyes glowed. "You don't say? Wow! Wonderful." Then she frowned. "I guess we better make every minute count. She put all the food back in the basket and set it on the floor. Then she pushed off the bed to the floor and sat with her head against the side of the bed.

"Now, for being so good, you get a reward." She pulled him off the bed facing her and opened her mouth. "Sweet cock, I want to eat you up, to suck you all the way. Come to me."

He had to bend just a little, then she had captured him and slipped his hard tool into her mouth and held it. She took more and more until he felt totally engulfed.

She bobbed her head and he began a gentle stroke. She began to hum a little tune. It was bizarre, it was wild, and it drove his passion so high so quickly that it took only a half dozen strokes before he climaxed. He kept his thrusting to a minimum so he wouldn't hurt her.

She took his second load and swallowed and came off him licking him clean and grinning. Morgan had fallen on the bed panting and feeling half dead from the explosion. Slowly he recovered and looked at her.

"Willa, you are one hell of a good woman. A fantastic bed partner."

"I'm only good when my lover is so fantastic! I'd like to keep you in my suitcase and bring you out when I need you."

"Given the chance, I'd wear you out in a week."

"What a way to die," she said.

She raised herself from the floor and began to collect her clothes. "I've got to go. Really I do. This was fantastic. I'm going to knock on your door every night at midnight and you better not have another woman in here."

Willa scowled at him and finished dressing. She went to the door. "If you leave your door unlocked, I might be able to come back. You stay right here." She blew him a kiss and stepped out the door.

For a moment he lay there, then he jumped up and opened the door silently a crack and looked out. He could see down the hallway to the left. The first thing he saw was the guard in front of the Senator's door. Then he saw Willa. She said something to the guard, looked back toward his door, then slipped into the Senator's room.

Morgan closed the door softly and snorted. She had been pumping him for what he knew. Now she was reporting—*to Senator Perridale?*

What the hell was going on here? Willa was a plant to seduce him and grill him for what he knew. Damn! He found an extra pillow and an extra blanket and quickly made a dummy form under the covers on the bed so it looked like someone was sleeping there. He left his hat on the cast iron bedpost and his gunbelt around the foot bedpost.

He pushed his Colt into his belt and stepped to the door. Out a narrow crack he saw the guard in front of the Senator's door. Damn! He waited and checked again. The guard turned and said something, then nodded and went into the senator's room. The door closed.

At once, Morgan slipped out of his door, closed it softly, and hurried down the hall two doors to room 211 and tried the knob. Unlocked. It was Willa's room and he knew she wasn't in it. He pushed inside and closed the door gently. The guard at the stairs was no longer there either. Good, he might go off duty at midnight.

Now all he had to do was wait and see what developed. He guessed that Willa would not be back to her own bed that night. She must work for the Senator. He sent her ahead to North Platte to find out what anyone knew who might be investigating the robbery of the satchel of railroad papers.

Must be. She pumped him for all he knew about it. He just hoped the false information he fed her got through to the Senator. His big break coming tomorrow should stir the old man into action.

Morgan looked around the room. Willa had even left a lamp burning low on the dresser. The room was full of Willa Porterfield. He smelled her perfume. Her undergarments were scattered over the bed. A small trunk was open across the room. A dress draped the chair.

That looked like Willa's way of living. He opened her door a crack and looked down the hall. The guard still wasn't outside the Senator's room. It might be a long wait.

An hour later Morgan still watched. He had thrown the dress off the chair and moved it so he could sit as he watched the corridor through the inch-cracked door.

One large kerosene lamp lit the hallway. It was about in the middle leaving huge shadows on both ends. A door down the hall opened and a man dressed in black came out. His hat sat low shielding most of his face. He walked to the lamp, turned the wick down and blew it out.

Morgan tensed. He heard the man coming toward him, tapping the wall, evidently counting the doors. A match flared at Morgan's room, then the knob turned and he saw the door thrust inward silently. Another match brightened the doorway, then the thundering sound of twin blasts from a shotgun battered through the hotel.

Then there were footsteps running.

Morgan bolted from Willa's room running after the man. He went down the hallway into the closest stairs. Morgan was less than twenty feet behind him. A lamp on the ground floor showed a man in black pants and jacket, gray hat. He fumbled for a six-gun at his belt but Morgan had his Colt pressed against the gunman's neck before he drew his iron.

Morgan pushed him out the back door of the hotel, pulling the bushwhacker's weapon from his holster and dropping it in the alley.

"What the hell?" the man growled.

"Hell is where you're heading, mister. I'm the guy they told you would be in that bed back in room 210."

"Oh, god!"

"About damn right!" Morgan held him by the back of his jacket and rammed him down the alley, then across the dusty street to the next alley and stopped behind a closed saloon.

Morgan spun him around and slammed him against the saloon frame wall. "Who paid you to kill me?"

"Damn, can't say. He'd kill me sure!"

"Might, I will for certain. You've got nothing to lose. Who paid you?"

The man didn't answer. Morgan slammed his gun butt down on the man's shoulder, breaking the bone from the shoulder to the breast bone.

The scream from the man wailed into the night. When it trailed off, Morgan's deadly, even voice asked again.

"Who paid you to kill me?"

"Dunno who he was."

"You ever see a white man after the Comanches finished having their fun with him? He dies, but it takes them four to six hours to do the job. Is that what you want? I know all the Comanche tricks."

"God no!"

"Who paid you?"

"Dinas, only name I know."

"Who is Dinas?"

The man didn't reply. Morgan hit him with his big fist, his knuckles smashed into the gunman's left cheek, breaking half a dozen small bones, slamming him along the wall until he fell to his hands and knees.

Morgan kicked him hard in the chest and he flopped over on his back.

"Who is Dinas?"

"A sleazy bastard."

Morgan kicked the bushwhacker in the side hard and heard a rib break. He hated a killer who worked from ambush. A real man stood up and called you out and gave you a chance. He enjoyed beating on this man. The bastard deserved to die for what he did. Him or me. He had his try.

"Dinas. . . ." the man on the ground said softly.

Morgan squatted down to hear. He put the six-gun muzzle under the man's chin and waited.

"Dinas . . . works . . . for . . . Senator Perridale."

"Thought so," Morgan said. He pulled the trigger. The booming shot in the North Platte night shattered the silence, and brought silence of another kind to the bushwhacker. The round traveled through the thin flesh under his chin, into his mouth and exploded with deadly consequences through the top of his mouth and into his brain.

Morgan snorted, stood and kicked the body once more.

"Bastard," Morgan said softly. "You got what you deserved."

As he walked back toward the hotel, he thought nothing about the man he had just killed. He didn't matter. He had played his hand wrong and lost. Every for-hire-killer should know the chance he's taking.

The Senator. Figured. Willa, too. She reported to the Senator and his bed gets blasted. He'd never see her again. If he did, he'd have to kill her too. And the Senator, and Dinas. That would take some doing.

Had to be done. They knew the chances, they lost, they all three had to die.

Chapter Eleven

Lee left the dead bushwhacker in the alley and slipped quietly back to the Nebraskan Hotel. He went in the back door and listened. He heard nothing. When he checked the second floor he found the Senator's guard gone.

No sheriff, no one in the hall, the door to his old room still wide open. He slid inside, collected his gear and went across the hallway to 211 and tried the door. Unlocked. Inside, Willa's room was as he had left it. He threw her clothes on the floor that had been on the bed and locked the door, pushed the chair under the knob and stretched out on the bed.

No one would know he was here. He wanted a few hours of sleep before tomorrow. That could be the time he had a showdown with a man named Dinas, Willa and the Senator. No wonder the man needed guards if he went around blowing people away with a double barreled shotgun.

The next morning he was up with the sun, took his gear down the back stairs and stashed it in the livery. Then he waited outside the cafe until Marleen opened. She smiled brightly at him.

"Good morning! You're a good surprise. A nice way for me to start the day. Come in. You want the surprise breakfast?"

"Surprise me, yes."

"Come on back and help," she said, smiling at him over her shoulder. "I should tell you I only let my favorite people into my kitchen."

The small kitchen was immaculate. Two wooden cookstoves, two woodboxes with split wood. Cabinets along one side holding supplies, and a long counter behind the stoves for mixing, baking and serving. On one wall was a needlepoint that read: "Home is Where the Heart is." On the other wall was a tintype picture of a soldier in a frame.

She saw him look at it.

"My husband," she said. Then she began making breakfast. "Today the special is flapjack sandwich. Ever had one?" When Morgan shook his head no, she continued.

"I bake the flapjacks big and thick, then have a layer of crisp bacon, another flapjack, a layer of two or three easy over eggs, another layer of pancake and another egg on top surrounded with four patties of sausage."

She smiled at him. Her green eyes checked him quickly. "You seem a little glum this morning." Her close cut black hair swung out as she charged around the kitchen.

Morgan sat on a high stool watching her. He liked her tall, slender form, and had to grin at the way she took charge of a kitchen and got the four items all cooking at once.

"Glum? Probably. It's this damn job I'm on. I'm getting nowhere and being shot at." He told her about the shotgunning last night in his former room.

"Just lucky I was out of the room at the time."

"Oh, dear! Did you tell the sheriff?"

"Nope. I like to take care of things like that myself." He jumped up and helped her with the bacon as she was working on the flapjack batter.

"The special costs fifty cents and I offer seconds, but I've only had one person who asked for seconds. I tell the customer if they ask for seconds they have to eat up the next plate full or they have to pay for that one, too."

Morgan forked the finished bacon out of a big cast iron skillet into a warming pan on the back of the stove and watched her making the flapjacks. Each one was eight inches across and a half inch thick.

As she began making the special for him, Morgan was sure he would not want seconds.

"Oh, I forgot to heat up the maple syrup!" Marleen wailed. She pointed to it on the shelf and Morgan put a glass jar half full in a pot of hot water and set it on the front lid right over the firebox. Soon the hot water was boiling.

A few minutes later, Morgan stared at the special breakfast on a twelve inch plate where it sat in front of him at the counter. It was a monster. With the first bite he discovered that the flapjacks had chopped walnuts in them.

He had never had such a good breakfast in his life. He was halfway through when Alexis Savage slid into a chair beside him at the counter.

"Thought over my deal yet, Mr. Morgan?" Savage asked.

"Still the same answer."

Marleen came out and walked up to Savage with a cup of coffee. He thanked her, looked at the stack of flapjacks and shook his head. "Two hotcakes, two eggs and some country fries." Marleen nodded and left.

"Look, Morgan. I know you're a good man with that gun of yours. I need some backing." He moved closer. "I'm ninety-five percent certain I know where the satchel is but I need somebody with me, backup. There could be some trouble, but I don't think so. We move in during dark, get the goods and slip out."

"Where is the place?" Morgan asked.

"Can't tell you. This is the best shot you'll ever have at finding that satchel, believe me. I've been pounding my head against this stone wall for three months. Come with me and you've got a chance."

Lee worked on his stack of cakes and bacon, eggs and sausage. It could be a chance he shouldn't pass up.

"If I go and if we find the goods, what then?"

"Then we decide. No use planning that now."

Morgan finished the special and worked on the coffee. Marleen brought out Savage's breakfast.

"You want seconds?" she asked Morgan with a twinkle in her eye.

"Not so you could notice. Great breakfast!" He slid a half dollar piece across the counter.

"Thank you, sir," she said.

When she left, Savage watched Morgan. "You going to come with me, or not?"

"When would we leave?"

"Two hours before sundown, today."

"I'll meet you at the livery at about five o'clock."

Morgan left the eatery and walked down to the Sheriff's office. As soon as he entered the office the lawman growled.

"Damn, you still alive?"

"Mostly. You see my room from last night?"

"Two rounds of double ought buck from a sawed off weapon. Damn good thing you weren't in that bed."

"Just wanted to let you know the body is still

working. Somebody else won't be if I catch him."

"Don't suppose you'd know anything about a gent who got his head blown off last night?"

"Don't suppose. Shotgun, too?"

"Six-gun by the looks. Same result."

"Violent town you have here, Sheriff. I best be going. Lots of business today."

Morgan went back to the livery, got out his carpetbag and changed into jeans and a heavy buckskin shirt with fringes on the sleeves. He rented a Henry repeating rifle from the livery man along with fifty rounds of ammunition. Then he found a spot in the haymow and caught up on his sleep. He was ready at five when Savage rode up.

They turned north out of town and Morgan looked at the former Pinkerton Agent. "We going to Indian Country?"

"Near the edge of it. You worried about red skins?"

"Worried enough to be cautious. Cautious enough to still have all my hair. You heading for Schoolboy's band?"

"Right again. There's an old woman there who I damn well know has the satchel. She's Young Fox's mother. The town Indian was in on the robbery, even you got to admit that. Where would he hide the goods? Safe in Indian Country. Who would he trust with it? His old mother."

"What happened to Young Fox?" Morgan asked.

"Happen? He's dead, of course. He hasn't shown up at the Sioux band and he sure as hell ain't in town. His partners in the robbery murdered him, way I figure, to shut him up."

"So why will his mother show us where he hid the goods?"

"She will or I'll slit her bloody throat."

They rode a while, then the question that kept gnawing at Morgan came out. "You speak Sioux, or does the old woman talk good English?"

"Neither one. She'll understand."

It was dark when they rode up near the Sioux village. Morgan knew where the fifteen tents were and where they should leave their horses before they worked up to watch the camp. When the camp activity quieted an hour or so after they arrived, they moved up toward a tipi that had a fox sketched in charcoal on the side. Savage had insisted that was the old woman's tipi.

Silently they worked as close to the tipi as they could, crawling the last fifty feet. Then they stood and walked to the conical dwelling as if they belonged there. They bent and went in the flap and found only a small fire burning in the center of the tipi.

Savage brought out a small torch he had soaked in kerosene before they left town. He lit it at the fire and held it high. An old woman woke up suddenly from a floor bed at one side. Savage moved to her and pushed a knife against her throat. She was the only one in the tipi.

"The satchel, the satchel," Savage hissed at her, but the old woman stared straight ahead not understanding. Savage tied her hands and feet, then the two of them looked everywhere in the tipi for the black leather case.

They lifted up the buffalo skins that formed the top of the tipi and were folded inside at the bottom with boxes set on them to keep out the wind and the cold in winter. They searched the ground but found no soft place where something had been buried. Every parfleche was emptied, every buffalo robe shaken out. Nothing was left untouched.

They didn't find the satchel.

"It's not here," Morgan said. "Let's get out of here while we still have our hair."

"She knows where it is, I'm sure she does!"

"You want to get Schoolboy over here and ask

him to translate for you? Come on, stupid, let's leave."

"I'll show the old crone!" Savage snarled. He took the torch and set some buffalo robes on fire next to the edge of the tipi. The old woman wailed.

"Let's go!" Morgan said. "Someone will see the fire in a minute."

Savage drew his pistol as they started out the flap. He turned and fired two shots at the old woman who was still tied up. He missed. They both ran out of the tipi into the darkness and headed for their horses.

The shots brought a dozen warriors out of their tents. Morgan saw a form dart in front of them and his Colt came up and fired. The form fell away and they charged past. By the time they got to their horses a hundred yards from the first tipi, they heard shouts behind them and the pounding of horses' hooves.

"You stupid bastard!" Morgan bellowed at Savage. "Why did you shoot at the old woman? That probably cost us our lives!"

They rode south as fast as they could through the dark night. Twice they found Indians ahead of them. Twice they both used their rifles and drove the riders back and rode on. The last time they fired, one of the Indians took a rifle round in the chest and plunged off his horse.

That stopped any further chase.

They rode for an hour galloping for a half mile, then walking their mounts, then galloping again. When the big dipper showed that it was nearly midnight, Morgan held up his hand and they both stopped.

"They aren't chasing us anymore, let's take a breather," Morgan said. They got off their mounts and Morgan grabbed Savage by the shirt front and blasted a hard right fist into his jaw. Savage went down to the ground, stunned by the sudden attack.

"What the hell was that for?"

"For lying to me. You didn't know where the satchel was."

"Thought I did."

"Then that asshole move when you shot at the old woman. Doing that inside a hostile Sioux camp is committing suicide for god's sakes!"

"I was mad at her."

"Right now I'm mad at you. You tell me everything you know about this case. Who you suspect, everything."

"I can't do that."

Morgan drew his Colt and shot Savage in the arm. The round missed the bone, tore through both sides of his arm and out. Savage sprawled on the ground screaming in agony.

"Everything you know, right now, Savage, or you'll never see the sunrise."

"Okay! God, you're a wild man! Okay, let me tie this arm up and I'll tell you. You know most of it now. I think Lame Charlie is in this up to his armpits. I think he planned the robbery. Young Fox and Shorty probably carried it off because Lame Charlie would be too easy to identify.

"Somehow the Sioux are involved. Probably Lame Charlie and Young Fox hid the goods in the Indian Country. I don't know where. I don't know what happened to Young Fox but he's probably dead. I also think that Marleen Forrester is involved somehow."

Morgan stared at the man still wrapping up his left arm. "Is that everything you know about the case?"

"Yes. I don't think any of the railroad people are mixed up in the robbery."

Morgan lifted his .45 and fired. The round went two inches from Savage's head and he swallowed in fear and fell to one side.

"I should kill you, Savage. You led me on a wild

chase and almost got me killed in that Sioux camp back there, and all for nothing."

He fired again a foot from Savage. "I think it's time for you to get on the train tomorrow and get out of town. I don't want to see your ugly face around North Platte again. If I do, I'm going to gun you down. You understand?"

"Christ . . . yes. I'll go."

"Mark this down as your lucky day—the day you should have died but instead you stayed alive."

Morgan mounted and rode away. He didn't want to even ride back to North Platte with the likes of Savage. The trip helped him in no way. It might have got rid of Savage, but that would be little aid in unraveling the mystery.

Where the hell was that satchel?

Chapter Twelve

Morgan had arrived at the livery well past one A.M. and after unsaddling his bay, he crawled into the maymow and slept. With morning he had shaved in cold water, washed up and headed for breakfast at Marleen's.

He growled at her when he arrived and she laughed.

"You sound just like my father used to." She set a big cup of coffee in front of him "Come on now, just a small smile. Life isn't all that bad."

Morgan grinned then. "I could stand some cheering up. You got any more of them hot cakes? Bring me a stack and a heap of bacon."

Marleen soon brought his hot cakes and scurried back to the kitchen. She was busy now with the morning rush. Twenty minutes later things eased off and she sipped at her cup of coffee beside Morgan at the counter.

"You work this hard every day?" he asked.

"Work hard? This is easy compared to trying to ranch. I've built fence, branded calves, helped in a roundup and worked a small trail drive up here from Texas. Now that is hard work. No wonder I couldn't get pregnant." She looked at him quickly. "Did I embarrass you by saying that?"

"Not in the least. Fact is fact. But I did think what a lucky man your husband was." She swung a dishtowel at him and laughed.

"I hear talk that the railroad big shot is coming in today in his private car."

"Johnson is coming here? He'll be treated like a king. After all, this is a railroad town."

"Railroad right down to the tie spikes and it won't change much for fifty years."

"You staying at the hotel?" she asked.

"No. I'm not giving them another chance at my hide."

"I've. . . ." She stopped. "Oh, damn!" She looked around. No one else heard.

"Don't say it if you don't want to, Marleen."

"I do want to, it's been so long. What I'm trying to say is that I've got a spare room in back where my cook used to live. It's safe and no one will know you're there." She hurried on then. "The rent's not too high and it comes with free breakfast. . . ."

"I'll take it. Bring in my gear after it gets dark. Then nobody will know—and nobody can talk."

"Oh . . . I never even thought about that."

"One thing though."

"What's that?"

"I don't wash dishes."

Marleen laughed and Morgan went back to his breakfast.

An hour later he watched the special train roll into town. It held only a steam engine, a private car, and the caboose. The private car was longer than a passenger car, had some windows blocked out and people who had seen the inside said it was all set up like a fancy house, with living room furniture, a bedroom, a kitchen and a dining room.

Morgan stood watching the car when a man in a suit dropped off the step and walked toward him. He wore no weapon Morgan could see. The man smiled as he stepped up to Morgan.

"Mr. Lee Morgan?"

Lee nodded.

"Mr. Johnson says he'd like to have you come to a special meeting here at the car in a half hour."

"I can be there."

The messenger touched the brim of his hat and hurried on toward the main street. Morgan stopped by at the Platte General store and bought a box of .44 rounds and a nickel's worth of hore-hounds. The little candies were one of his favorites.

At the appointed hour, 8:30 A.M., Morgan stepped into the private rail car of railroad millionaire Quenton Johnson with a watchful eye. It might be the only time he had a chance to visit such a rail car. Just inside the door was a small entry room with a bench-like seat richly up-holstered. There were cut glass lamps set in holders in the walls, and a tapestry on one wall and oil paintings on the others.

The man in the black suit greeted him. "Mr. Johnson will be with you in a minute. The others are down here."

They went into the next room. If Morgan didn't know better he would think he was in a fancy home. This section of the car was fifteen feet long with four upholstered rocking chairs that would swivel toward the windows or turn toward the center. At the far end of the section, a wide sofa was built against the wall with a moveable uphol-stered chair beside it.

The roof of the car was lifted higher than most cars and had fancy decorative metal work in bright enameled colors.

Each of the windows was four feet square and with rich heavy drapes that could be pulled to shut out the sunlight.

On the floor was a thick carpet that was well padded.

Morgan stepped into the area and saw that Wild Bill Nelson was already seated in one of the fancy chairs staring out the window. In the next thickly upholsterd swivel chair sat Lame Charlie Bard. Both watched Morgan come in, showed no surprise, and nodded in recognition.

Quenton Johnson came boiling into the room from the other end of the car five minutes later. He carried a sheaf of papers in one hand. The man in the black suit was with him with a yellow pad and a pair of sharp pencils.

The railroad's president still looked like a chiseled block of granite. His full head of dark hair belied his 55 years. Only the slight twist of his nose where it had been broken and not set, gave his appearance a touch of warmth.

He looked at each of the men and sat down in the fourth chair which he swiveled around to face the others.

"We're talking about the goddamned patent deeds. We've got 400 sections of land deeds missing. Newspaper man, you say you know where they are and can get them?"

"Yes, sir, Mr. Johnson. In my investigation of the story I dug up some facts and know for certain where the satchel is hidden."

"Where?"

"I'm sorry, I can't tell you that until we work out an agreement."

"Figures. What the hell you want for them?"

"No, not ransom, Mr. Johnson. I only want a fee

for helping you recover them. I want you to sign over one quarter of the deeds to me for my services."

"Sounds like ransom to me."

"No sir. I don't have them in my possession, I only discovered where they are hidden and legally that's a payment, not ransom or blackmail. My lawyer assured me of that."

"How far are they and what do we need to supply you to get the deeds," Johnson asked, his face now harder, more stern than before.

"I'll need a force of ten riflemen, mounted. It's about half a day's ride each way. The ten riflemen and anyone else you wish to send along to protect your interests."

"That's your deal?"

"Yes sir."

"Please step outside and take a walk. Be back in five minutes. I want to confer with my experts."

Lame Charlie stood and limped to the door and soon it banged shut. Johnson turned to the man in the black suit.

"Legally, is he right?"

"Close enough. Be hard to win a case against him claiming a felony of either the actual robbery, of theft or conspiracy to defraud."

"Morgan, you've been on this a few days. How do you read him?"

"Everything I've been able to dig up so far points to Lame Charlie as being one of the men deeply involved with planning and carrying out the original robbery. I can't prove it yet, but it seems almost sure. If he does know where the papers are hidden, I'd say you can prosecute him for armed train robbery and murder as well."

The granite face did not change. Johnson turned his glance toward the fourth man in the room. "Wild Bill?"

"I don't trust the little asshole. I'd say Morgan pegged him just right."

"Mr. Johnson," the suited man said. "Bard will want an agreement in writing. We can give him an agreement, but with a clause if he was involved in the robbery it is null and void. It'll be in the body of the agreement he'll never read."

"If he does turn up the deeds, Lame Charlie will have a small 'accident' on the way home and not get back alive," Wild Bill said.

"I don't want to know anything about that," Johnson said. "If you get the deeds, be sure Lame Charlie doesn't get any of them." He turned toward Lee. "Morgan, you bring back the patent deeds and your deal will be completed satisfactorily. Let's get it done today. Ira, write that agreement now."

"I'll get at it," the man in the black suit said. "We'll leave within the hour. Mr. Nelson, can you arrange to hire ten men with their own rifles and revolvers for the ride within an hour? You and Morgan can count as two of them."

"Hell, yes," Wild Bill said. "I can get you twenty out of the saloons. I need eight, right. Take me a half hour. Meet you at the Livery."

"I'll be along as an observer," Ira said. "Mr. Johnson has other important meetings, one with Senator Perridale. That will be all, gentlemen."

They all stood and Wild Bill hurried out first. Morgan hesitated and turned back to Johnson.

"One more thing, Mr. Johnson. When you talk with Senator Perridale, be cautious. Right now I'm betting that whoever stole those patent deeds, was somehow deeply involved with the senator."

Both men looked up sharply.

"What facts do you have?" the lawyer asked.

Morgan told them about the Senator's ownership of the newspaper and his suspected tie with

Lame Charlie and how the woman set him up for murder after trying to pump him for everything he knew about the case.

Johnson growled. "Never have liked that fat little bastard. We'll be on our guard with him. This is getting more complicated than I first figured. Good work, Morgan. Now see what you can get from this newspaper man today."

Less than an hour later the rag tag detail left from behind the livery. Morgan still had the Henry repeating rifle. The man in the black suit, Ira, had not changed. He rode along at home in the saddle despite the string tie, suit and the black low crowned hat on his head.

Lame Charlie liked to ride. It made him equal with the rest of them. He moved up and down in front of the men like an army general. Ira had talked to him, given him the agreement and they both signed it and he let Lame Charlie keep it.

Then they rode. Lame Charlie and Ira were in the lead, the rest of them came behind in a column of two's more out of convenience than any organized effort.

They turned north out of North Platte, but then angled sharply to the northeast. Morgan moved up beside Lame Charlie.

"You can tell us where we're headed now, Charlie," Morgan said.

"Hell, why not?" The newspaper man had a large grin on his face. He had the agreement that would make him a rich man. A hundred sections of Nebraska farm and ranch land!

"We're going to a small stream fifteen miles out where the Schoolboy band had a camp about three months ago. That's where the goods were hidden. I had a long talk with Schoolboy White Eagle. He told me he talked with Young Fox and this is the spot where he buried the satchel. All we have to do is go out and pick it up."

Morgan heard but didn't believe. Schoolboy would not tell the newspaper man where the goods were, even if he knew. Morgan doubted the educated Indian knew their location. Schoolboy had more than a few thoughts of using those grant deeds somehow for the benefit of his people, the Sioux, who he said owned this land, not the government, and certainly not the Union Pacific railroad.

Morgan wondered if Schoolboy had set up a trap for Lame Charlie, or if this was just a cloud of smoke to conceal what Schoolboy was doing to find the satchel?

They rode for two hours, took a break and then in another hour were at the small stream. It was no more than fifteen miles from town, but well west of the present spot where Schoolboy's band camped.

Wild Bill stationed the eight riflemen around the small camp site in a circle of protection, then the four men rode into the spot where the grass was cropped low and an area along the stream showed a number of worn places were tipis had stood and many feet had trampled the grass down.

Lame Charlie rode around the site looking it over carefully. He frowned as he came back to the others.

"Supposed to be a lightning struck cottonwood," he said. "Not a single cottonwood here, nothing tall enough to take a good lightning strike. Just a bunch of willow and brush."

"Maybe it's the wrong spot," Wild Bill suggested.

"Hell no, this is the place. Look at the tipi circles. They camped here, damn certain."

"What besides the tree are you looking for?" Morgan asked.

"Two standing rocks near the stream, half a man tall on the east side."

They rode along the stream for a hundred yards. There were no rocks of that size on either side of the creek.

"What else?" Wild Bill asked.

"Well, damn! He said the rocks were twenty paces north of the lightning struck cottonwood, and six paces due west from the rocks they buried a big iron cook pot with the satchel wrapped tight in a buffalo robe. Down about two feet."

Will Bill laughed. His strange cackle slanted through the brush and brought grins to the other men there except Lame Charlie.

"Son, you been flim-flammed by an expert. You done bought a piece of goods that ain't there. Schnockered as my old German friends used to say. Bamboozled. Son, you ain't got a pot to piss in here. Hell, we're dead here, we might as well head back for town."

"No. No, by damn! It's here. Schoolboy assured me as an educated man and a gentleman that it was here. The tree could have been chopped down!" He rode up and down both banks of the small stream but found no stump.

For half an hour he scoured the area. The other three men sat on the grass, drank from the clear, pure little stream and then smoked cigars that Ira furnished them.

"So much for this try," Morgan said. "One more damn dry water hole. When are we going to find some a spot with some water?"

"Hell, these damn injuns ain't that reliable," Wild Bill said. His brows went up. "Hey, maybe. . . ." he stopped. "Naw."

Wild Bill got up and walked over to his horse, mounted and rode to Lame Charlie. They seemed to be talking as they rode along searching for something that Morgan figured simply wasn't there.

"Let's head back," Ira said. The man in the black

suit reset his hat grimly. He adjusted something in his vest which Morgan figured was a derringer.

The two men mounted and rode out to where Lame Charlie and Wild Bill talked.

The little army had ridden a half mile back toward town when Lame Charlie turned and rode west. Wild Bill pulled his six gun and fired a round in the air.

"The two of us are moving out in another direction. Wouldn't pay for any of you to try to follow us. Just keep moving back to North Platte."

"What the hell you doing, Nelson?" Ira asked, his hand close to his vest.

"What the hell it look like?" Wild Bill asked and motioned them forward with his pistol. They rode on toward town, glancing back now and then. Wild Bill now had out the rifle and monitored their movement until they were out of sight of each other.

Chapter Thirteen

As the men rode back toward North Platte, Ira turned to Morgan.

"Why did Nelson leave? Where are they going?"

Morgan pulled his mount to a walk and the others around and behind him did the same.

"Why? Because he tried the waters here and decided he didn't like them. He figures the other side is going to win, and he thinks he can make more money there. Simple."

"What made him change his mind?"

"He could have had the same idea I did. It's possible that Young Fox did hide the satchel, that sounds reasonable. The cottonwood with the lightning blaze and the two rocks may exist but if they do, they're at another Sioux camp ground. The plains Indians have to move around often because they don't want to kill the grass in one spot for their ponies to eat, or to kill down the game to a level where it can't reproduce.

"So Wild Bill suddenly decided the satchel might be hidden at another camp the Sioux made, only this one six months ago?" Ira asked.

"Yeah, right."

"So why didn't we go with them?"

"We'd have a gun battle on our hands, for reason one. And reason two is they might find such a camp and the landmarks, but the satchel isn't there."

"But Schoolboy said. . . ."

"Exactly. I spent three hours with the man a few days ago. Schoolboy White Eagle is intelligent, bright, sharp, knows both the Indian ways and the white eye ways. He lied to Lame Charlie."

"Why would he do that?"

"To gain time so he can find the papers on his own. He knows exactly how valuable they are. The second reason he lied is that he's afraid of Lame Charlie. The man carries much more power in Nebraska than we know. It could be his close tie to Senator Perridale."

Ira shook his head. "I thought this was going to be a simple matter."

"When you deal with the Sioux, nothing is simple."

They rode faster then. Suddenly, Morgan was anxious to get back to the cafe before it closed. He was hungry, and he wanted to talk to that pretty, nice, intelligent lady. Also he had a small errand to run as soon as it got dark.

They arrived back in town midway through the afternoon. Morgan put his mount away in the livery, then picked up his rifle and carpetbag and went through the alleys to the back door of Marleen's restaurant.

She heard him come in and stepped into the storeroom with a .32 caliber revolver in her right hand. When she saw him, she grinned and lowered the muzzle.

"Glad it was you," Marleen said. "I've never shot at anyone before. Not sure if I could."

"I'm the one who's glad that you didn't shoot. Dinner still on the menu?"

"Sure, anytime. Let me show you where you can drop your gear." She led him through another door into a section of the building that wasn't used. In one corner was an iron bedstead with mattress and springs, a small dresser and three chairs and a table.

"My cook used this before I realized I couldn't afford him. He moved on. I guarantee nobody will try to shoot you in here." She paused. "It might be better if I brought your meals back here instead of you eating out front, okay?"

"Fine. I got a hunch there's a couple of gents out there who'd just as soon see me in Boot Hill." He grinned and she smiled back. It was a great smile and it fascinated him. He had to remind himself this was not just another woman like Willa. Marleen was a lady.

She paused as he dropped his gear on the bed. He noticed it was made up fresh.

"Thanks . . . for all of this. I don't know. . . ."

"You hush up. There's water and soap and towels. I'll have a snack for you before supper. A surprise snack. You'll have to take whatever I can find." She grinned as she hurried back to the kitchen as the tiny bell on the door signalled that a customer had come in.

After the thick roast beef sandwich, piece of pie and cup of hot coffee she fixed for his snack, he spent most of the time in the kitchen, watching Marleen, talking to her. He found out she and her husband had come out from Pennsylvania to homestead. They had a good start but she couldn't prove up on the land alone for the last four years, so it went back to the government.

They talked about his work, and soon he was pouring out the details, asking her opinion on the patent deeds robbery.

"So it looks to me like Lame Charlie is more and more my prime suspect. He seems to be convinced that the satchel is hidden on Indian lands. To me that means he was in on it, that he knew Young Fox hid the goods, either without telling him where, or the Sioux moved the satchel after they both hid it."

"You said the Pinkerton man, Savage, thought the Indians had it as well. Any idea why he thought that?"

"He didn't tell me. Just a logical sequence, I'd guess. Tonight I'm going to have a man-to-man talk with Senator Perridale. Maybe I'll get some new information."

She looked up, surprised, then worried. "You be careful. You said you thought he hired someone to try to shoot you. Should you be going to see him at all?"

Morgan smiled. How long had it been since he had known someone who seemed sincerely worried about his safety. It was a warm, good feeling.

"I'll be safe enough. I just hope it's a warm night."

For supper that evening Marleen served him a bowl of baked beans with side dishes of cooked cabbage and bacon, mashed potatoes and gravy and a big slab of tender ham.

"Enough?" she asked as she came and looked at his clean plate and bowl.

"Plenty," he said. When she reached down for the dishes, he caught her hand. "Marleen, I don't know how I can say thank you to show you how I feel. I appreciate all of the extra trouble you've gone to for me."

She held onto his hand when he was ready to let

go. "Lee, it's a pleasure, really. It's been a long time since somebody used this room." She smiled gently. "It's also been a long time since I've felt relaxed and comfortable around a nice man."

She took the dishes and left quickly.

Morgan got into the hardware store by the alley door just before it closed and bought what he needed: 40 feet of half-inch rope. When he went back into the alley it was dark. He walked to the back of the Nebraskan Hotel and climbed the metal rungs of the ladder to the roof and sat down against the still sun-warm black roofing and waited.

For a while he snoozed, woke up and checked his watch with the flare of a single match. Ten minutes to midnight. He'd slept longer than he thought. Morgan went to the front of the hotel roof and counted the windows. There were eight rooms across the front. The Senator's was the last one, the corner room.

He tied the rope securely around a brace on the two-foot false front over the corner room and dangled the line down the front of the hotel. He tested the rope, then went over the top and worked down the rope hand-over-hand, his feet firmly against the outside hotel wall.

Morgan saw he was between the windows. Good. He moved to the left and saw that the Senator's window was open to help cool down the room. There was also a light on. Morgan held the rope tightly, pushed off from the building the way he used to push away from the tree on his back-yard swing, and angled away from the building.

When he came back toward the hotel he kicked to the side, then swung directly through the Senator's open window and dropped to his knees in the Senator's room.

A light glowed from two coal oil lamps. The big

bed was filled with naked arms and legs intertwined.

"What the hell?" the Senator's voice barked.

Morgan stepped to the bed and put the blue muzzle of his Colt against the Senator's forehead.

"Hell, now that's a nice place to visit, furniture salesman, but you're not going to like living there."

The woman turned her head.

"Top of the evening to you, Willa. You do enjoy your work."

Senator Perridale began to sweat. He hadn't moved a finger since he saw the gun at his head. Willa began to roll away.

"Stay where you are, Willa," Morgan said softly. "Let's get two things straight. One, before I leave this room somebody is going to be dead and cooling off fast unless I get the right answers. There could be two dead bodies here. That wouldn't bother me a bit."

"Morgan, be reasonable . . ." Perridale began.

"I'm reasonable. You tried to kill me in my bed. You missed. It's my turn. Isn't that reasonable?"

"For god's sake, Morgan. . . ." Willa began.

He moved the blue muzzle until it pressed against her lips.

"Ever see a body after a bullet has gone through teeth, then into the brain and out the top of the head? Make even you look like hell, Willa. You shut up!"

He moved the weapon back and pushed it in the man's ear.

"Now, Senator, we were discussing fairness. Isn't it fair that I get a try to kill you?"

"Yes. Sounds fair. But I'm against it."

"Talk and save your skin. You own the local newspaper and the newspaperman. Did you put him up to robbing the train to get those patent deeds?''

"Swear, Morgan. I don't know nothing about that robbery.''

"No? You saw Anderson, Batchelor and Roundale get rich by stealing millions in the railroad stock scandals. The Credit Mobiler was done and gone so you figured out a new way to swindle the government and the railroad. You might not make two hundred million, but half a million would be plenty for you, for a time.''

"I don't know a thing about it, Morgan. I'm just trying to build a rail line to Utah. I'm on the transportation committee. Use your head, Morgan. I can be a big help to you.''

Morgan heard the sound, a small click, but enough. The Senator was talking too loudly, too much. Morgan spun. His Colt blasted a round at the door just as it slammed open and a guard stood there with a pistol. Morgan's first round hit the Senator's guard in the upper chest and slammed him back against the door jamb. He kept lifting the six-gun and Morgan's second shot drilled a neat hole through the man's forehead. He jolted against the wall and then slumped to the floor.

Willa screeched and fainted.

Senator Perridale pushed her off him and sat up.

Morgan went over and slammed the door and threw the bolt. He waved the six-gun at Perridale.

"The man died in a fair fight. Self defense. You should be the next one. If anybody so much as frowns at me in the next few days, I'm tracking you down and blowing you balls off, Senator. You understand that?''

"But. . . .''

Morgan stopped him with a flick of the Colt's muzzle.

"I'm sure the governor would be interested in knowing how many other newspapers you own around the state. Hear my warning or you'll be an ex-senator—in prison."

Morgan looked out the window. The street was a ribbon of black, with a splash of light from a late night saloon here and there. He could see no one on the street below. He grabbed the rope, tested it, then went out the window and hand-over-hand to the street below. He landed in the total darkness of the alley.

A few minutes later he pushed open the alley door into the cafe building. A light glowed ahead in the kitchen. Marleen came from the kitchen with a lamp, hurrying toward the door.

"Oh, Morgan! Good, it's you. I was so worried. I heard some shots."

She stood there in her flannel nightgown, her green eyes wide with worry and surprise. The nightgown fitted tight around her throat and came to her ankles. Marleen smiled at him. "I'm glad you're safe."

"Marleen, you're beautiful standing there with the lamp that way."

She smiled. "I'm not embarrassed. I thought I might be." She caught his hand and lighted the way into his room. She put the lamp on the small dresser and sat down on the bed.

Then she stood quickly, pushed down the bedspread and turned down the near side of the bed. She slipped under the covers and tried to smile, but it was forced.

"Oh, damn, Morgan. I was going to be so brave, even brazen. I was going to seduce you." She laughed softly. "You know me well enough to know that's not my style." She held out her arms. "Please, Mr. Morgan. Please, right now. It's been such a long, long time for me."

He sat on the bed and looked at her. She was a

vision. Slowly he bent toward her and kissed her lips lightly. Her hands came up and held his face. He kissed her again and she sighed.

"You know I can't stay in town, be with you. I can't make a commitment."

She nodded, tears in her eyes.

"You should also know I didn't plan this. I know that you're a real lady. I warned myself not to try to get familiar with you. You're so damned pretty." He bent and kissed her again.

"Morgan, I've dreamed about something like this." She sat up and let the covers fall. She had slipped out of the nightgown. Her hand-sized breasts were bright with blood-flushed areolas. She grinned.

"Not very big, are they? But I've never had any complaints. I want to undress you."

She began with his buckskin shirt. "Yes, I'll marry again, soon I hope. A nice young rancher. Then I'll go back to a ranch and work fourteen hours a day, get old and tired and wrinkled before my time, and have six kids and die by the time I'm forty-five, the way most ranch women do.

"Every day for the rest of my life, I'll remember tonight. I know you won't. Women are different. When I was trying to get pregnant, a friend told me to make love once a day for the whole month, and I could't miss. We did, but I still didn't get pregnant and my Wally lost twelve pounds."

She smiled and pulled at his pants after he had taken off his boots.

"I want you all bare, totally naked, and I want to turn up the light and stare at you like a thirteen year old girl. Damn, but it's been a long time!"

She concentrated on getting his pants off and then the short underwear. As it came down, she stopped.

"My god! It s been a long time. A man's cock is the most marvelous instrument in the world.

Oh . . . glory! She lay down on her back and lifted her knees. "Would you believe that I've only made love in one position? My Wally used to call it the missionary. Do me different."

Morgan rolled over on his back and lifted her over him.

"Me up here?" she asked. "Will it work this way?"

Slowly, tenderly, with more compassion and love and care than he had felt in many, many months, Morgan made love to Marleen. It was a night that *he* would never forget. Marleen had been wrong about that.

Chapter Fourteen

Morgan woke up with the sunlight in the strange bed. Marleen's head nestled against his shoulder and one arm lay across his chest. He felt a warm satisfied glow this morning. That was damn dangerous for a fiddlefoot like him. He lifted her hand and kissed her fingers, then lay it across her bare stomach.

Gently he slid out of the bed without waking her. Her face in repose was still beautiful. She was the kind of woman a man wouldn't mind being tied down to. He dressed, then bent and kissed her lips.

She responded at once. "I've been awake watching you. It's been a long time since I've seen a man dress."

He sat on the bed and put his arms around her. They kissed softly, then again.

"Oh, dear. I'll be furious when you leave. I

warned myself you were a man on the move. It didn't matter." She reached up and kissed his nose. "Last night was so wonderful. I can't describe it for you. That was my first time since Wally died. You were worth waiting for. Even if I can have you only for a few days and nights, it'll be worth it."

She squirmed out of his arms, still naked. "I've slept in. I won't even have the fire going by breakfast time!"

Morgan sat there grinning. "Now it's my turn to watch you dress." He pulled her to him and kissed both her breasts. She pushed away.

"Later, Mr. Morgan. I can promise you that there won't be much sleeping done here tonight."

Then she was a flurry of clothes as she dressed and rushed to the kitchen. By the time she got there, Morgan had built a fire in both kitchen stoves and warmed his hands. Marleen came in and quickly set up the kitchen for the morning customers. Then she went and opened the front door and let in two of her regulars.

Morgan had ham and eggs and country fries, and by eight that morning reported to the private railcar as ordered.

Johnson was up and puffing hard on a big cigar.

"No damn satchel, Ira told me yesterday. I'm mad as hell at Wild Bill. The traitor switched sides. I want you to shoot down the bastard."

"I didn't sign on to kill people. You want him dead, hire yourself a paid killer."

Johnson looked at him sternly for a minute, then grinned and nodded. "Told Ira you wouldn't do it, not in a cold blooded shooting at least. So instead of killing him, find out what they did after they left you yesterday. Learn what they discovered. You told Ira that Schoolboy lied to Lame Charlie. Maybe you better have another talk with that educated Indian. If he knows more than he's told you, try to make a deal with him."

"I know what he wants. Land for his people."

"Can't happen. Indians aren't even citizens. Can't vote, can't own property."

"I'm going to need something to bargain with. How about a twenty section parcel set up legally as a reserve, owned by the Union Pacific, but granted in perpetuity to the Sioux Indians for their exclusive use."

"I'll talk to Ira, sounds possible. How about ten sections instead?"

"How about forty? Schoolboy claims his band owns all of this land, a million acres across Nebraska and Kansas. He won't help us if he gets the deeds for only ten sections."

"Twenty. See what you can do."

Morgan left and prowled the town looking for Lame Charlie. He wasn't in his box car. It was closed with a brand new padlock. The news man must have had to cut the old one off. At last, he found Lame Charlie under a cloth in the North Platte Barbershop.

Morgan sat down in a chair and looked at the paper, then when Lame Charlie looked up, Morgan grinned.

"I hear you had another long ride for nothing after we left you. No broken top cottonwood, no pair of waist high boulders."

"How you know that?"

"It's all over your sour expression. You feel like a man who had a fortune in his hands and let it slip through."

"What do you mean by that?"

"Whatever you want it to mean. You might tell Wild Bill to watch his hindside. Johnson is mad as a wet pussy cat."

"Wild Bill can take care of himself."

"Yeah, I agree, but can you, Charlie? That's the question."

Morgan walked out of the barbershop. He'd found out what he wanted to know. They had found nothing at the next Sioux campground along the little stream. Lame Charlie was stalled in a box canyon.

Morgan's next move was a ride to see Schoolboy White Eagle. It would have to be another night time entry. He was getting good at it, but this time he figured they would have some guards stationed around the camp.

Morgan headed toward the alley when a voice stopped him.

"Where you going so fast, white eyes?"

Morgan turned slowly. Wild Bill stood thirty feet away, hands at his sides.

"Hear you've been riding an empty trail, Wild Bill."

"Sometimes. Now looks like I hit paydirt. You see, you and me are on different sides of the coin now. You're fair game. There's a bounty on your head, you hear that?"

"Not lately. Since when are you a bounty hunter?"

"Since a thousand dollars. That's more than I make in two years, normal. It's a cowhand's wages for four years."

"So shut up and draw," Morgan said.

"Soon. I'm figuring. You're fast, I heard. Not as fast as Frank Buckskin Leslie, but fast. So do I let you have first draw, or do I go for you from this distance and take my. . . ."

Morgan knew about first draw. It gave the man who moved first that split second advantage. If he was as fast as the other gunman, first to draw wins. If not, whoever shot the straightest was still alive.

Morgan's hand came up like a streak, caught the butt of his Colt, pulled it out and lifted the muzzle in an aim and shoot sequence. His thumb drew back the hammer and he stroked the hair trigger. It all happened in less than a quarter-of-a-second.

He had ajusted for the thirty foot distance, aimed as always at the man's chest, his heart, and fired in one rapid, smooth motion that came only after thousands of rounds of practice.

Wild Bill knew he had talked too long. When he saw Morgan's hand start to move, he slapped leather as well. He was fast too, maybe as quick as Morgan on the draw. The muzzles came up and fired.

Lee Morgan felt the sting of the bullet, the jolt as the big slug slammed into his flesh. It staggered him, spun him half around, but he watched the other man.

Wild Bill's hands lifted skyward as Morgan's round hit him. His six-gun came free of his hand and Wild Bill's eyes went wide with surprise, then the fire died and they stared without seeing. The .44 round had sliced through Wild Bill's chest cavity, tipped sideways when it nicked a rib and plowed through his heart as it tumbled. The big man died before he hit the dirt there on Main Street.

Morgan saw a few people gather on the boardwalk. He turned and moved into the valley, then ran through it and vanished into the back door of Marleen's cafe. He got to the kitchen just as somebody ran in the cafe's front door.

"Shoot out down on Main Street!" the man shouted and ran out again. Three of the eaters left their food to run to the scene.

Morgan looked at Marleen. Sweat beaded her forehead and she wiped a drip off her nose as she worked over the hot stove. Then she saw the blood on his side.

"You were hit," she said calmly. "Nursing time.

Come on." She led him to the side of the kitchen where she had a drawer with medical things for burns and cuts.

"Accidents happen in my kitchen," she said. She pulled his shirt out of his pants and lifted it. The round had hit him in the side and bored through an inch of flesh.

"Missed your ribs, might have nicked something inside, can't tell. At least the lead went on out. Nice clean little wound. You know about antiseptic?"

Before he could answer she sloshed grain alcohol over the two wounds.

Morgan bellowed in pain.

"Don't be afraid to yell if it hurts," she said. "That kills the bad germs or something, and makes it heal better." She put some salve over the bullet holes, then taped on some white square pads she had sewn up and had available, and finally wrapped a long strip of sheet around his stomach to hold the bandages in place.

"Now, get two days bed rest and come see me again," she said. Then she rushed back to the stove to save a steak from over-cooking.

"I don't want to hear about it, but I'm glad the other guy almost missed."

"I've got to take a ride, and this looks like a good time. Going out to see Schoolboy. Won't be back until morning. Keep a light on in the window."

She motioned to him and he went to her. She leaned up and kissed his lips twice, then three times. When she eased away she smiled. "That will keep me going until you get back. A lady has to have some sustenance."

Morgan slipped out the door and had no trouble getting to the livery without attracting any attention. He saddled up and rode out, the Henry repeating rifle in his boot. He'd find a shady spot along a creek and have a nap. It was much safer for him out here now than in town, and he couldn't get to the Sioux camp until after dark.

He wondered who had sicked Wild Bill on him? Could be Lame Charlie, or the Senator, or whoever else it was who had tried to kill him twice before. Morgan found his creek about an hour north, got off his bay and stretched out on the grass.

He gasped at the quick pain in his side, then it was gone. Tomorrow it would hurt like hell. He had a four hour nap and woke up eager to get on to see Schoolboy.

Now he had some bargaining power. He wondered if Schoolboy would trust the railroad to honor such a pledge. As far as Morgan knew, it had never been done before. Looked like a good spot to start a new plan for this band of Sioux.

Four hours later, Morgan slipped through the flap of Schoolboy's tipi. Only two women and two children were there. He had his Colt out and motioned for them to stay back.

The younger woman edged forward. "You here before," she said in halting English.

Morgan nodded. "Talk with Schoolboy."

The woman nodded and chattered something to the other woman who put down the knife she had been holding under her skirt. The younger one showed him where to sit in front of the small fire.

"Schoolboy soon," she said.

The leader of the band came into the tipi a half hour later and smiled when he saw Morgan.

"I see our security is not much better than before. One of our scouts did find your horse. I recognized it as yours. Welcome to my humble home."

He turned to the older woman and spoke in the Sioux dialect.

"It would be my assumption that you were here to talk about the missing patent deeds in the satchel. Were you involved in the attack on Young Fox's mother a couple of days ago?"

"I came with Alexis Savage to talk with her. The gunfire was his, not mine, and totally unnecessary."

"You also went to one or two of our former campsites yesterday. I, too, think the papers may be somewhere near where we camped before. But in which place?"

"Schoolboy, I have talked with the president of the Union Pacific railroad, the boss. I've worked out a deal with him that I think you'll like. All you have to do is help us find the satchel and return the deeds. When you do, the railroad will give to your Sioux band a grant of twenty sections of land here in western Nebraska."

"But I am not a citizen. No Indian can own land. How can he do this?"

"I'm not a lawyer, Schoolboy. He said he'll have his lawyers draw up the agreement, a codicil attached to the deed, that the twenty sections of land shall be owned by the Union Pacific, but may not be sold or used by the railroad. These twenty sections of land may only be lived upon, farmed, ranched, or otherwise used by the Sioux band known as Schoolboy's band, and any other Sioux he permits on the land."

"I wish I had studied law at the university, but it sounds right. I'll want to have my own attorney go over the papers before I sign them."

"Fair enough. He used the term in perpetuity, which is legal talk for forever."

Schoolboy sat crosslegged in his blue denim pants and no shirt and stared at the fire. "For many years I have dreamed of some way to save the land my ancestors called home. This may be a way to save a small piece of it. Twenty sections, twelve thousand, eight hundred acres. A mere speck of land compared to what the Sioux have ridden over for generations."

Both men sat watching the fire for five minutes, then the older woman brought bowls of hot soup for them and they ate. When the food was gone, Schoolboy took out an eighteen inch long ceremonial wooden pipe and slowly filled it with tobacco.

"We will smoke the peace pipe, between us. This shows that we agree, that our solemn oaths have been given and can be changed only by our mutual consent."

They smoked, and Morgan was surprised at the strong taste of the tobacco.

When the pipe had been taken away by the younger wife, Schoolboy stirred the fire.

"Now that I have some incentive, I will find out where the satchel was hidden. I have known that Young Fox, the town Indian, did take part in the robbery. A white man helped, then was paid off and rode away.

"Lame Charlie met Young Fox and the courier and they rode toward Indian Country. The white man cut off the courier's hand, then killed him and took the satchel. Young Fox then took Lame Charlie into Indian lands and together they hid the satchel.

"If Lame Charlie can't find it now, it must mean that Young Fox feared for his life and went back alone and changed the hiding place. But before he could make Lame Charlie understand this, the newspaper man killed Young Fox. Now he can't find the satchel."

"Someone must know. Would Young Fox tell his mother? Who?"

"I will find out. You are right, someone must know. Young Fox was a man who loved to brag. He has told someone in my camp. I will find out."

He stretched. "It's late. Stay the night and

tomorrow I'll ride part way back to town with you."

Morgan grinned. "Sorry, my new friend. I have a late appointment with a very important lady."

Schoolboy smiled. "I understand. Here I can have the best of both worlds: two wives. I'll need two days to find the hiding place. A braggart always tells his good news. Someone knows, but does not understand how important it is. I'll contact you when I know. Are you at the hotel?"

"No, come to Marleen's cafe, have a cup of coffee and tell her you want to see me."

They shook hands, then Schoolboy led Morgan past the guards to his horse and he rode south toward North Platte.

Chapter Fifteen

Morgan rode back to North Platte as quickly as was practical. He pulled in at the long end of two A.M., stabled his horse and walked into the back door of Marleen's Cafe that was just off the alley.

A light burned in his room. Morgan locked the alley door behind him and went to look.

Marleen sat in a rocking chair near his bed. She had a book in her hands but had leaned back in the chair and slept soundly. She was fully dressed.

Morgan smiled, then kissed her lips softly. She murmured in her sleep and smiled. He kissed her again. Her hands came up to his face. Then she was awake.

"Hi sleepy face," Morgan said.

She smiled, kissed him hard and then stood up. "I've done as much sleeping as I want to do tonight. That is, if you're not too tired."

She kissed him again and led him to the bed.

That night the lovemaking was better, more tender than it had been the night before.

The next morning, Morgan had breakfast and moved out on his next mission. He wanted to be sure that he knew everything that Lame Charlie did about the robbery. He would assume he knew a lot of things he didn't and see how the crippled newspaper man reacted to the statements.

It was press day.

Morgan came into the box car and surprised the thin printer on the mechanical side of the shop.

"You! Morgan, you should be in jail right now for killing Wild Bill."

"Self defense. Thirty people saw it. How can you plead self defense for gunning down a one handed courier named Casper Gorman?"

Lame Charlie moved to put the press between them. "Don't know what you're talking about."

"Young Fox's mother said her son was working for you. She told us you planned and led the raid on the train, but couldn't do the actual robbery, so you hired that drifter, Shorty Wilberton, to do the robbery with Young Fox."

"An Indian's word ain't worth anything. Everybody knows that."

"Means a lot in the Schoolboy band. They all are mad as hell. Want to come in and get you and toast your brains over a slow fire. I told them I'd help. Said I'd drag you out to the edge of town and tie you spread eagled in the sun. Then I'd cut your eyelids off so you couldn't close your eyes. The sun will burn your eyes blind in two hours."

"Get out of here!"

"Or what? You'll chop off my hand the way you did Gorman's?"

"I never did that."

"I've got witnesses who can prove you did the whole thing. The Senator told you when the messenger was coming. You set up the robbery, then killed Gorman. You made a mistake on Young Fox. He wasn't as dumb as he looked."

Morgan began moving slowly toward the printer. He was staring at Morgan but not really seeing him. Then Morgan made a dive and caught the printer's arm as he started to jump away.

Morgan brought the man's hand down and forced it on the large piece of newsprint on the press, directly below the heavy pressure plate.

Lame Charlie screamed as he saw Morgan start to swing the lever that would smash down the heavy weight, crushing his hand flat between the metal plate and the newspaper metal type below it.

Morgan stopped the heavy weight just as it touched flesh.

"Now, let's talk about Gorman. Who cut off his hand with the axe?"

"The Indian. I told him to cut the chain in half."

"Who shot Gorman?"

The silence stretched out. Morgan let the lever move a little bringing a scream from Lame Charlie.

"Stop. Okay, so I kind of shot him. What could we do with him? He could identity us both. I had to shoot him."

Morgan heard something at the box car door and looked up. The six-gun blasted three times. Morgan ducked as lead slammed through the air beside where he had been standing. Lame Charlie screamed as the lever Morgan had been holding back fell into its proper place, smashing the heavy plate down against the paper to print another sheet. Only this time, Lame Charlie's hand was in the way until it was mashed down almost paper thin.

Lame Charlie's scream was cut off suddenly and Morgan wondered why. He grabbed the lever and pushed it the other way. As the weight came off Charlie's hand, he dropped to the floor next to the press.

Morgan looked down and saw two bullet holes, one in Charlie's forehead, the other in his chest. He drew his Colt and looked over the top of the press at the box car's door.

Someone stood there, leaning against the metal. He couldn't see a gun. Morgan jumped forward and covered the person standing in the sunshine brightness coming through the door.

Then he saw it was a woman. He moved closer and noticed a six-gun, a big .45, hanging in her hand and pointing straight down at the floor. He moved up and took the weapon out of the woman's hand.

She turned and looked at Morgan. The woman was Holly, the dance hall girl he had talked to about Gorman three or four days ago.

"The bastard deserved to die," Holly said. "Thanks for helping me. I heard him confess, I executed him. You can tell the sheriff if you want to." Holly turned and walked down the wooden steps and headed for town.

Morgan hurried after her. "Holly, listen to me. We'll go tell the sheriff what happened. I'll back up your story. I'll walk you there right now."

She looked at him and he knew she didn't care one way or the other. He nodded. "It's the right thing to do, Holly. The sheriff will understand. You shot down a murderer and a train robber. He won't even file charges."

Morgan led her up the alley nearest the sheriff's office, then down to the door and pushed it open. The sheriff looked up, surprised.

"Sheriff Lewis. This is Holly. She wants to tell you something."

Holly looked at him. He nodded as Morgan

placed the six-gun on the counter.

"I just shot Lame Charlie Bard. He's dead."

Sheriff Lewis stood and came to the counter.

"Why did you do that, Holly?"

"Because he confessed that he robbed the train and then killed Kasper Gorman, the railroad courier."

Sheriff Lewis looked at Morgan.

"True, sheriff. I was talking to him, grilling him, and Holly must have followed me and heard him confess. She shot him before I knew she was there."

The sheriff looked back at Holly. "You can really shoot that big gun?"

She nodded. He put a can from his desk on a chair at the other side of the room and handed her the revolver. "Holly, I want you to shoot that can off the chair."

Holly looked at Morgan, who nodded. She picked up the weapon, held it in both hands and aimed down the barrel and fired. The can spun off the chair. Morgan brought back the can. The bullet hole was dead center.

"Justifiable homicide, I think they call it," Morgan said. He took the weapon out of Holly's hand and put it on the counter. "Any more questions for Holly, Sheriff?"

"Not now. I'll write up some papers for both of you to sign. We've been losing citizens fast here lately. What are we going to do for a newspaper now?"

"Ask Senator Perridale, he owns the paper. I'll take Holly back to her place."

Morgan walked Holly to the saloon and told the barkeep what happened. He nodded. Morgan went out the back door to the alley and down to the cafe. He told Marleen about it. She was nodding when he finished.

"I know exactly how she feels. Will she get in trouble?"

"I don't think so. Not if we can prove some other way that Lame Charlie was in on the killing."

Morgan relaxed. "Now all I have to do is wait until I hear from Schoolboy. I got a hunch it won't be long."

Marleen was deep into the noon rush but managed to whisper, "Why don't you stay right here to do all that waiting," and grinned.

Word that the newspaperman was dead passed quickly through the small town. Senator Perridale glared at one of his guards. This was too much.

"Go bring in that detective, what was his name? Savage, yes, get Savage in here right now."

Savage had not left town when Morgan had insisted. Instead, he had offered his services to the Senator who was getting short on good men and accepted him.

"Savage, can you find Morgan for me? He isn't staying in the hotel or at any of the boarding houses. I don't know where he is, but he has to eat somewhere. He might be camped along the river. Get out of here and find him. His head in a bucket is worth a thousand dollars to you, and I'll be glad to pay it.

"I don't care how you do it, or where or who helps you. Just find the gunsharp and kill him. Today if possible, the sooner the better."

"Yes sir, I know this town pretty well. Have a few ideas where he could hide out and still eat. I saw him the other day over at. . . ."

Senator Perridale interrupted. "Enough! I said I didn't want to know. Now get out of here!"

The Senator scowled and slammed his hand against the wall. "Damnit! How is it possible that I have surrounded myself with such a band of incompetent assholes!"

Willa looked up from where she sipped at a beer and ate from a tray of cold cuts and bread and different relishes. "Of course that doesn't include me, does it, Stanley?"

"Damn right, it includes you! You messed up from the very start. Didn't find out a damn thing." He snorted. "Now I want you to get your clothes on and get out there and help find Morgan. If you see him before the other guys, you get him in your bed and push a knife between his ribs. The way we planned. He's too dangerous running around loose. After what he did to Lame Charlie, we've got to be damn careful."

"All right, all right. It just seems such a waste. He's really a good looking guy, and he's wild in bed, and . . . well, I'm sure he could be convinced to work for you. . . ."

"Enough! Out of here, you floozie. You nail his ass to the wall and chop it up in little pieces or you don't need to come back!"

"My, my. You're sure in a bad mood today."

"Bad mood?" He swung at her but she jumped back out of he way. "The whole plan is coming apart. My retirement is going out with the tide, and you talk about me only being in a goddamn bad mood?"

Willa dressed quickly, putting the dress over the three petticoats she wore, then a little matching jacket. She primped in the mirror, then tried again. "I'm not happy about this," she said.

Senator Perridale growled at her and she ran toward the door which she closed quickly as she stepped into the hall.

Willa sighed. She either found Morgan or looked for another job. She would try to find him, but she really had no idea at all where to look.

Chapter Sixteen

Schoolboy White Eagle sat in front of his tipi fifteen miles above North Platte. His shield and lance stood beside his tent flap. His bow and three arrows leaned against the shield. It was in the traditional manner. He could be ready in an instant to defend the clan. The women worked on hides from three recently killed buffalo.

The old ways, the life of his father and his grandfather, must still be followed in day-to-day living if the Sioux wanted to continue as a nation.

But the young men must also think in terms of long range plans. What would the tribe be like in twenty years? Fifty years? What was his responsibility to his small band? There were fifteen warriors, fifteen family units.

He knew the Sioux nation must forget war, the people must settle on one piece of ground and become planters, farmers, ranchers. They must learn to manage the land, not let nature manage them. Easy for him, a man in two camps to say. His white eye training and schooling told him one thing, but his native Sioux blood urged him to stick to the traditional ways.

Schoolboy stood and went to the lodge where Walks Alone had moved in with her younger sister. Walks Alone was Young Fox's wife. She had borne him two sons before he went to the white eye's town to live. Only after he had been missing three months did she declare that he was dead and went to live with her sister and become third wife to Running Bull.

The tipi flap was in place, and Schoolboy stood outside the tipi waiting to be asked to enter. Soon one of the women saw him and Running Bull came out at once. They talked of the hunt, of how many more would be needed to fill their parfleches with jerky and pemmican for the long winter ahead. Then Schoolboy asked if he could speak with Walks Alone.

"She is still sad about her husband," Running Bull said. "I tell her she is needed here. Her sons are now my sons, but she is still third wife."

He brought out the woman, in her late twenties, and left her alone with Schoolboy. She sat in the grass in front of him and looked up.

Walks Alone was not a pretty woman. Her features were askew and the side of her mouth tipped down. But she was a hard worker and good producer of babies in a people who did not excel at childbirth.

"Walks Alone, the time for mourning is over. Life must go on. I'm pleased that you have found a tipi where you are wanted and needed."

She only nodded.

"When Young Fox came back to our camp that last time, he carried with him a small bag, a satchel made of leather. Do you remember it?"

"Yes. I hoped it had beads in it for me, or some cloth, or perhaps a white eye dress."

"Did it?"

"It was tightly closed with bands of iron."

"Where did Young Fox hide the satchel?"

"He didn't. He told me to hide it for him, so he could not be tortured into telling the spot. I hid it that same night when the moon came out round and full."

Schoolboy tensed. He might have found a way to help out his band, his people.

"What camp were we at then, Walks Alone?"

"The Birdwood camp. I remember it because it is the last good sized stream we camped on this summer. It was deep enough that I helped the boys splash and swim in the water."

Schoolboy sat down on the grass near Walks Alone and looked away. He didn't want to rush things. Above all he didn't want Walks Alone to think her role here would be overly important. She must remember she was only a woman.

Schoolboy lit a cigar with a match and watched Walks Alone studying him. She was curious. He puffed a moment, then went on.

"You say you hid the satchel after Young Fox brought it to you. Do you remember where you hid it?"

"Yes. Young Fox told me never to forget where it was. He said it was valuable. He said it would buy us ten tipis and a hundred horses!"

"Where did you hide the satchel, Walks Alone?"

"Twenty paces east from a dead tree by the stream, then ten paces north."

"How did you hide it?"

"I wrapped it in a buffalo robe, then put it in a large white man's bucket and buried it with the bottom up two feet under the soil."

"Can you find the same place again?"

"Yes. My husband told me to remember."

Schoolboy nodded at her response and sent her back into the tipi and told her to ask Running Bull if he could come out and talk.

The two Sioux warriors sat in the shade talking of the glories of the past, and wondering what the future would bring for the Sioux.

"The time is almost here when the white eyes will control us, will defeat us at war and force us into small areas of land and order us about. They are many, we are few."

"The Sioux will fight until every warrior is dead!" Running Bull growled.

Schoolboy shook his head. "Then there would be no warriors to protect our women and children. Would you leave them to the ravages of the white eye? There is a better way. A way to spar and talk with the white eye and get what we want—enough land to live on in peace and not lose all of the old ways."

"If it is possible," Running Bull said.

"The secret may be at our Birdwood stream camp. Your third wife buried something there. We must go quickly and find it. Can you bring her tomorrow and ride to the old camp with me?"

"If it is important."

They left the next morning just after nine o'clock. They would be taking a path almost due west from their current camp. The Birdwood River ran into the North Platte River about twenty miles west of the confluence.

There was no real hurry, the only one alive who knew where the satchel was buried was with them. Still, Schoolboy struck out at a faster than usual pace.

Back in North Platte, Lee Morgan grew

impatient waiting for Schoolboy. After most of the first day sitting around the back room of the cafe, he decided he had to go back and see the Sioux white Indian. The next morning. He left at six just after daylight.

Morgan hadn't noticed the interested cowboy down in the barn saddling his own mount. He had been there watching—the way the Senator had ordered him. He rode quickly to the hotel and knocked on the legislator's door.

A half hour later, Alexis Savage and three men with rifles had been rounded up and were hot on Morgan's trail. They spotted him in the flat land, and stayed well behind him.

Back at the hotel, Senator Perridale had a hunch that this was the time for action. He called in his last bodyguard and sent him to the saloons and to the street to round up ten men with rifles who could ride and weren't afraid of a little hot lead. He would have a double surprise for Lee Morgan!

Morgan rode with an urgency he didn't quite understand. Schoolboy said he would come and tell Morgan if he learned anything important. But there was nothing to do here and Morgan was bored. He was sure that Young Fox had bragged to someone, and that Schoolboy would find out where he hid the goods.

He was almost to the Indian camp when he saw three Sioux on horseback riding west. One of them was a woman. He came closer and hid in some brush as they passed. Schoolboy led the trio.

Morgan considered joining them, but held back. Instead, he trailed them from back aways, sticking to cover whenever he could. They had no reason to think they were being followed.

It was another three hour ride. The Indians rode quickly and when they slowed it was to ride into a thick brushline along what Morgan figured was a good sized stream. This could be a former camp-site, perhaps the one they were at six months ago when the robbery took place.

He faded upstream, then entered the brush and tied his horse. He took his Henry repeating rifle and walked silently along the water. A half mile down he found the campsite. It had a large open area with little brush and a few tall cottonwoods. He could see the effects of the camping but it was quickly returning to its natural state.

At the near end of the open area he saw the three Indians. The woman was pacing off from a dead snag beside the stream. She stopped, turned due north and walked again, then she pointed at a spot and Schoolboy began to dig with a white eye shovel. He worked for five minutes, then shook his head.

The Indian woman went back to the dead snag and paced it out again, turned north and walked. This time she came up several feet farther. Again Schoolboy used the shovel.

This time the digging was easier. He pushed the shovel in the ground in several places, then dug. A minute or two later, the metal shovel hit some other metal in the ground. Schoolboy gave a little shout of delight.

Five minutes later, a large milk bucket was pulled from the soil. The woman knelt down and took out a piece of a buffalo robe, then from it unwrapped a black leather satchel.

Morgan grinned. She found it! The satchel was back in circulation.

Schoolboy took the satchel from the woman, and Morgan figured he was thanking them. They both went to their horses, waved at Schoolboy and rode off to the east.

The white Indian stared at the satchel for a moment, then put it on the ground and used the shovel to fill the hole and return the area to its more natural state. He took out his pistol and aimed at the satchel. Morgan guessed he was going to shoot off the locks.

Before he could fire, a rifle round drove through Schoolboy's left thigh knocking him down.

"Throw the weapon away from you and don't move or you're one dead Sioux!" a voice bellowed from the woods. Morgan had been about to lift up when the shot sounded. Now he kept in his hiding spot.

Schoolboy screamed something at them, then tossed his revolver toward the voice.

"Now, don't move," the same voice commanded. Savage and his three riflemen ran into the open ground, and Savage grabbed the satchel.

"I've got it! I did it! I'm a millionaire!"

He looked at the Indian on the ground. "Too damn bad about this, Schoolboy. Hell, I even like you. But you're excess baggage right now." He drew his revolver and turned toward the Sioux.

Morgan's shot from the Henry caught Savage in the chest and killed him in a fraction of a second.

Morgan shifted to his second target, the man closest to Schoolboy with a rifle. He dropped him with the second shot and the other two men threw down their weapons.

"Give up!" Goddamn, no more shooting!" one of the riflemen said. The other one dropped his weapons as well.

"Gun belts, too," Morgan barked, and the gunbelts and revolvers in them hit the ground. "Now get on your horses and ride out of here, as fast as you can go. I'll be throwing lead at you until you're out of range."

The man ran into the brush for their horses. Morgan watched them mount up and ride. He sent two slugs over their heads and made sure they kept moving.

Then he ran back into the clearing.

"Schoolboy, looks like I came along just about at the right time," Morgan said. "The least I can do is take care of that little nick you have on your leg."

Schoolboy smiled through the pain.

Chapter Seventeen

A chill swept down Morgan's neck as he looked around the cleared space beside the stream. It was too damn open.

"Can you walk?" Morgan asked softly.

"Hobble," Schoolboy said through clenched teeth.

"Better than shot dead. Somebody else is here. I'll grab the satchel and we dash to the brush, twenty feet up north."

They moved suddenly. A voice cried out in the brush. Three shots snarled at them but missed. They charged for the big cottonwood and the brush beside it.

"Oh, damn!" Morgan growled. He pulled Schoolboy into the brush and they crawled silently for twenty feet, then sagged to the ground.

"You get a nick, too?" Schoolboy asked.

"Somewhat, left shoulder. But I can still shoot.

How many of them you guess?"

"Three shot, one yelled. I'd make it at least six or eight. They weren't expecting us to move. Getting ready for a killing time."

Morgan sliced off the tail of his shirt and they bandaged both wounds. Both slugs had missed the bones.

Morgan looked out through the brush.

"Now we play Indian," Schoolboy said. "I'd guess you're good at it. We listen and we watch." He had been whispering. A moment later he reached for the Henry, made a rolling motion with one finger, then he tracked a shadow in the brush and fired. A scream of rage rang through the woods.

"Fucker shot me good!" somebody bellowed.

As soon as the shot sounded, both men rolled to the right. Three rounds slammed into the spot where they had been lying.

Morgan lay behind a fallen cottonwood log and lifted to look over it. He saw more movement and fired four times with his Bisley Colts. Two shots came in return.

"You really want a war, Senator? We have the prize. We wait until dark and leave."

"Wishful thinking, young man," Perridale said from behind a tree. "I still have eight strong men, all with rifles. You're short on weapons and ammunition. You both will die long before it gets dark."

A silence stretched out.

The Senator continued. "I could make a deal with you. The patent deeds should be in blocks of 20 sections each. I'll let both of you take four of the deeds each. That is good for 80 sections of land for each of you. In ten years it'll be worth a fortune.

"You throw out the satchel and when we see the

remaining patent deeds, you'll be free to go. Sound fair to both of you men?"

Morgan reached for the Henry and put two rounds into the thin outer bark of the cottonwood tree about head high.

"Damn you to hell!" the Senator roared.

"Don't like your deal, Senator. Don't we pay you enough? Tough to get a little graft in Washington these days, right?"

Two of the Senator's men ran from one cottonwood to the next. Morgan guessed their try to circle around them. He judged their next move and sighted in on the near edge of the tree. Both bolted at once for the new cover.

Morgan tracked one and fired with a small lead. The heavy .44 caliber round ripped through the runner's left side and exploded in his heart, dropping him into the brush. The second man made it.

When Morgan looked around, Schoolboy was gone. The shirt he had worn had been shucked free and lay on the ground. He must have moved to the right to work around the Senator. Morgan grinned and worked to the left.

He moved without a sound as if he were a huge cat. Before he put a hand or a knee down to the ground he made sure that there was nothing there that would make any noise by breaking or rustling.

After six feet he came to a cottonwood tree thick enough to cover his body. He stood up behind it and looked around the far edge of the clearing. A black, low-crowned hat bobbed along thirty feet away, moving toward him. It was the same hat the second man had when Morgan shot one of the two.

Or was it a trap?

Morgan watched it again. No trap. He slid down the tree to the light brush and concentrated staring through the foliage. He saw movement. Was it Schoolboy? No.

Wrong side. The figure moved again. Morgan raised the Henry and sighted in. A second later the black hat showed plainly in a void in the brush. Morgan did not know the face below the hat. He fired six inches below the face and heard the scream as his round hit home.

He dove to the left and then lay still.

There was no return fire.

Morgan furrowed his forehead. Why not return fire? Then he saw the reason.

Three men rose up from his flank and ran forward across the edge of the clearing. He fired, levered the Henry and fired again. Two of the men went down with leg hits. The third turned and ran back to the woods.

"You assholes are probably working for a dollar a day. Is that all you make to get yourselves killed? Get smart. Charge a hundred a day or run for town."

Morgan darted through the brush and beat the rounds fired at his voice location.

"Take off right now and I won't track you down. Leave the lying, cheating, fraud of a senator in his own juices."

"Morgan, you bastard!" Senator Perridale shouted. "I'll kill you myself!"

"Perridale, after today's over you'll be in one of two places—dead in hell, or back in Omaha selling furniture to little old ladies. Sure as hell the choice isn't going to be yours."

Morgan heard a shot to the left and a scream. That would be Schoolboy using his revolver to good effect.

Morgan crouched in the brush, every nerve alert. Someone was close by but he didn't know where. He could almost smell the danger. His eyes checked every tree, every bit of dense brush. He wouldn't move, the other man had to, to get a shot at him. He lifted the six-gun and slid in three rounds to fill up the six chambers.

A branch snapped to his left. He looked that way. Nothing. To his left again he heard a rustling and looked that way as a squirrel ran out, lifted on its rear legs, chattered at him in anger and looked around.

Then came a cautious step, a smashing of brush and a scream as a man leaped from behind heavy brush and fired at Morgan. The Colt came up and blasted three times. The shooter in front of him had been high.

Morgan was on target. He shot the man twice more in the chest. The man with dark red hair gasped and fell backwards clutching at the holes in his heart.

Morgan turned searching every direction as the sound of the gunfire faded. Soon it was gone. Morgan could find no more of the enemy. Some were dead. He was sure some left not buying in on the job to be killed. Where was Schoolboy and the Senator?

Morgan moved back slowly in the direction he had come from. He arrived just before Schoolboy did. They both looked at the satchel which they had left as they went on their killing runs.

"Any more of them?" Morgan whispered.

"Don't think so. Can't hear anybody but the Senator. He's behind a tree over there with an empty six-gun."

"And no army."

"True."

"Let's look in the satchel."

Schoolboy put the leather case four feet away and fired once at the first padlock. It danced halfway around, then snapped open from the force of the round. His second bullet tore the lock, still intact, out of the leather bindings.

Morgan motioned Schoolboy to the case. He opened it and inside they found the legal papers. Patent deeds, each one for a twenty miles long strip of land one mile wide and extending back from the railroad.

"Should be forty of them in there," Morgan said.

"We got them, now what do we do with them?" Schoolboy asked shaking his head.

"The Union Pacific made you an offer. I think that Johnson will stand by it. He's getting off lucky."

"But only twenty sections when my people owned millions and millions of acres over three states? He looked off into the distance.

"Are you going to kill me or not?" The plaintive voice of Senator Perridale came through the woods.

"Mostly that's up to you," Morgan said. "Throw out your six-gun into the clearing. Then walk out with your hands clasped behind your head."

Morgan and Schoolboy started a search through the brush to see if the men hit were dead and if there was another bushwhacker waiting for them to come into the open. They met on the far side.

"Nobody left on this side," Schoolboy said.

"My side's clean." Morgan tossed Schoolboy the satchel and they walked out to talk to the murdering U.S. Senator.

Morgan stopped six feet from the man. He had a bruise on one cheek. He had lost his hat, and his fancy coat was torn and dirty, but he was not wounded.

Schoolboy stood directly in front of him. "Senator, did you send Savage and his men after us?" the white Indian asked.

"Well . . . damnit, yes."

Schoolboy shot the Senator in the left thigh so

quickly he had no idea it was coming. Perridale screamed and went down in the dirt. He looked up at the Sioux, his eyes blinking back tears.

"Bastard!"

"At the university in Chicago, that's what we call evening the score, Senator. Any questions?"

"Damned savage!"

"Quite the contrary, Senator. I learned this form of justice in the sacred white man's halls of ivy and learning."

"I'll see you hang for that!"

"Senator, you're not in a good bargaining position," Morgan said. "Incidentally, we have the patent deeds. All of them. Your little swindle isn't going to work."

"You can't prove a thing."

Schoolboy produced a slender knife that looked sharper than a razor and held it next to the Senator's white throat. "Out here, frightened little man, we don't have to *prove a damned thing.*"

Morgan laughed. "Seems to me you're the one who tried to kill both us. You brought eight or ten men after us." Morgan lifted his Colt and aimed it at the Senator's left shoulder. I've got some evening up to do myself."

The Senator snorted. "You're not a savage, Morgan. You wouldn't shoot me that way."

The Colt exploded and the round jolted through the Senator's left shoulder. He staggered back, then fell into the grass.

"Hell, I feel evened up for now," Morgan said. "Course I don't know what Holly will do when she finds out the Senator here was partners with Lame Charlie. She'll get a six-gun somewhere, I'd say. That courier was her man. She was planning on marrying up with him."

"You can't do this," the Senator said between sobs. "I'm a United States Senator!"

"And I'm sure that body will glad to be rid of

you. I'd say it's about time to get back toward town."

They found their horses, grabbed the closest one for the Senator and pulled bridles off the rest of the spare mounts they found. They would wander back to town in a day or two looking for a free meal.

"Let's ride," Morgan said.

He still hadn't figured out what he was going to do with the patent deeds. An idea began to form in the back of his mind. It would take some time to fully mature, but there were several hours as they rode the twenty miles to town.

Chapter Eighteen

Morgan didn't think it was necessary to tie Senator Perridale on his horse. Where could he go? He did tie up the Senator's wounds with about half of his torn up shirt. Perridale protested but not after Morgan quit the wrapping and let the wounds bleed for another five minutes.

They rode to the river and followed it downstream. When the Senator realized where he was and how he could get back to town, he kicked his horse into a gallop and suddenly rode away from them as fast as he could.

Schoolboy on his fast little Indian pony surged out and caught the bigger animal after fifty yards. Schoolboy knocked the Senator off his horse with one punch. The Sioux slid down easily from his war pony and jumped hard on the man's right arm, breaking both the arm bones. Perridale passed out. When he came to, he was screaming in agony and fear.

"I'm a United States Senator. I want you to arrest that man," he kept screaming.

At last Morgan slapped him hard on the side of the face and he quieted.

They got him on his horse but did nothing to ease the pain on his broken arm.

As they rode for another hour, Morgan worked on his plan to get a chunk of that good Nebraska land. It wasn't as lush as Idaho, but he could start another horse farm. The damned deeds had to be legally signed over by the Railroad.

He could simply take two or three of the 20 section deeds, but then how would he get the railroad to sign them over? He couldn't.

Dammit! He had his hands on a half a million acres of prime ranch land, and there didn't seem to be much that he could do with it. He thought of every scheme in the big book on swindles but came up with nothing that would work.

He could urge Schoolboy White Eagle to hold out for 80 sections of land. But even so there was no way Morgan could get half of it back from the Indians. They wouldn't really own it. Damn!

A new idea came, a little horse trading. If the land was selling to settlers for $2 an acre out there in the ranching country side of Nebraska, a section would be worth twelve hundred and eighty dollars. Twenty sections would go for $14,400. Yeah interesting. He could offer Johnson a flat $10,000 for one twenty section chunk and simply hold on to it. He could have a little gold mine of his own and all above board.

Morgan saw Perridale glancing from side to side. Then he made another run for it, slamming into Schoolboy White Eagle's mount in front of him, half unseating the Indian and making his pony stumble and fall away to the side.

Morgan spurred after him, caught him after a quarter of a mile, just as Schoolboy raced up.

"I won't *allow* any more of this outrageous treatment!" Perridale bellowed. He lifted his arm and Morgan saw a derringer in his left hand. He fired. The round was close, but missed. In the next fraction of a second Schoolboy drew his revolver and fired.

The .45 slug creased the Senator's shoulder from the side, bounced off the shoulder bone straight ahead and hit his neck sideways. The powerful round tore a section of the vertebrae out of his neck and thudded to a stop against the far side of the skin on his neck.

The late Senator Stanwick Perridale slumped in the saddle, then lolled to one side. His head fell in the same direction and pulled him out of the saddle. He crashed into the Nebraska soil and rocks near the river on his head and shoulders, then crumpled to one side.

"Well damn," Morgan said. "I was hoping he'd have to stand trial."

"He would have talked his way out of it. All of our witnesses are dead." Schoolboy's scowl was intense. "He was an evil man, Nebraska doesn't need him. The Sioux nation certainly doesn't need him or his kind."

Morgan slid off his horse. "We got to make it look good. Like a robbery." They pulled the Senator's pockets inside out, stripped fifty-five dollars from his wallet and discarded it, and took a diamond ring off one finger and threw it into the North Platte.

"Should do it," Morgan said. "Now let's get to town and come in from the north."

They did, two hours later, tired and hungry. They tied up their horses in front of Marleen's Cafe, and gulped down coffee and steaks and then more coffee.

It was another hour before they went to see if the private railroad car was still on the siding. It was.

Quenton Johnson looked down at the documents on his desk and smiled. "At last, at last. It's not the cash money involved. I just don't want any shyster con man train robber out there to think that the Union Pacific is an easy mark."

He shuffled the patent deeds together.

Morgan shuffled his feet, then looked up. "Johnson, White Eagle and I have been doing some talking on the way back. Since the robbery involved the death of one of his band, we think that the reward to him for finding the deeds and compensation for the lost warrior and his own gunshot should be 40 sections instead of twenty. Those should be side by side. I'm sure you can arrange that."

Johnson looked up. "We agreed on twenty sections."

"You and I talked about twenty. I couldn't speak for White Eagle. He's got sixty people to think of."

Johnson turned to White Eagle, who now looked every inch a Sioux warrior. "I guess he better talk for himself. You said he understands English?"

"I do," White Eagle said. His enunciation was precise, his grammar perfect. "I did quite well actually, on the varsity debating team. We went to the regionals one year and I won every debate. As Mr. Morgan has stipulated, my suggestion is that you grant my wish for the 40 sections. As you said, it's only a few thousand dollars to you. It could be the salvation of half the Sioux nation."

Johnson sat down, stunned. Then he laughed. "I'll be damned! Schoolboy, you are something. Hell yes, we'll get the numbers changed. Forty sections it is. I checked with the Department of the Interior and they weren't a bit happy. Said I could do anything I wanted to with the land but I couldn't deed it to an Indian.

"This grant said when the order comes down to rout all Indians into their reservations, your group would have to go, whether you were on public or private land."

"I thought about that, Mr. Johnson. But the land will still be ours to use even if we aren't there. In perpetuity, I understand. We can set up a land company to rent or lease it out. Sooner or later we will be able to reclaim it. Perhaps it will be our grandsons or great grandsons, but it will be their inheritance!"

Johnson sat there and nodded. "Done, by damn. I like this young man. How would you like to come to work for the road? I'll put you on my personal staff. You can help me with Indian relations all the way to Utah."

White Eagle shook his head. "Respectfully I must say no to your fine offer, Mr. Johnson. I have my band of Sioux to watch out for. I must be a buffer between them and the white eyes."

"I understand." Johnson turned to Morgan. "You've still got a gleam in your eye, fast gun."

"That's land fever, Mr. Johnson. Decided I'd like to take part of my pay in land. I hear the going rate is two dollars an acre. I'll give you a flat ten thousand for a twenty section strip, right alongside the Sioux lands."

"That's a little under the going rate."

"But I earned it. You said that to you this land is only a few thousand dollars."

"Making this kind of business deal is not the way I managed to build this great railroad. But what the hell! I'll have our legal man get on that as well. A bank draft good for the balance to you will be ready tomorrow, Mr. Morgan."

The Union Pacific President grinned. "Now I'd suggest you two go over to the doctor's office and get those nicks and scrapes of yours fixed up and any assorted lead bullets dug out all proper."

They did.

When the two came out of the doctor's office, a parade of sorts came down main street. In front was a horse with a body draped over it. The man leading the horse stopped at the Sheriff's office and went in.

The lawman came out a few seconds later and stared at the upside down face.

"Lord A'mighty! Gonna be old Billy Hell to pay." He looked at the man beside the horse. "Who are you, mister, and how the hell did this happen?"

"Hey, I don't know. I was coming down from Ogallala on the river road and found him. His horse had wandered off. I tracked it for a ways, then gave up. Looked to me like he'd been beat up, then robbed and shot dead."

"I'd say that's about right. You know who this is?"

"Not a glimmer, Sheriff."

"This is our ex-United States Senator Stanwick Perridale. Damn but there's gonna be hell to pay." He looked up and down the street. "Well, stranger, you better come inside and write down everything you can remember about this." He grabbed a kid who was staring at the body.

"Boy, you go fetch the undertaker. We can't have the U.S. Senator hanging upside down dead on Main Street."

Morgan and Schoolboy White Eagle walked on to the cafe and closed the front door. Morgan hung the "closed" sign on it. The two men in the cafe soon left and Morgan, White Eagle and Marleen sat around the table in Morgan's room sipping coffee and making plans.

"By tomorrow at this time I'll be the proud new owner of twenty sections of Nebraska semi-hill country. Not too good for farming, but should be prime grazing land for beef. Now all I need is a manager to run the place. I'm not much for staying tied down to one spot for long."

"Ranch managers are easy to find," Marleen said. "Stop by at any saloon."

"Not my style. I'm choosier than that. I usually find a better class of manager in a cafe."

"Tough luck, you just closed me up," Marleen said.

White Eagle laughed.

Marleen looked at Morgan.

"You surely don't mean. . . ."

"That's exactly what I mean. You said you helped run the ranch. You rode fence, you branded, you kept the books, you were on a trail drive and a roundup."

"But *managing*, that's different."

"You'll learn. Tomorrow or the next day we go register our deeds with the county recorder in whatever county we'll be in. You'll have five thousand dollars cash money in the bank to get started with. I'll hang around to help you put up the ranch house, a small one at first. Then we'll need a bunk house and a corral."

"I don't know."

"Deals like this don't come along every day," Morgan said.

"You'd own the spread?" she asked.

"All twelve thousand, eight hundred acres of it. One mile wide and twenty miles long."

"And you want me to run it, manage the ranch?"

"She's starting to get the idea. I figure White Eagle here will be moving his band to its new land if there's a good water supply on it. We'll get back to Johnson tomorrow morning and pick out a good spot. We want water rights on the North Platte and a stream if possible. Maybe out on the Blue River somewhere."

"This is a lot to think about all at once."

"Way I figure it, with fifteen to twenty good riding men right next door, you should be able to train them to be cowboys as you need more men."

White Eagle grinned. "Yes, some of our young men would like that. It would give them something to do. You could pay with beef and blankets, maybe even small houses eventually."

"Stranger things have happened," Morgan said. "The fact is, I think your hard riding Sioux men would make outstanding cowboys."

"It sounds too wonderful to be true," Marleen said. Tears welled up and spilled down her cheeks. She put her arms around Morgan and let the tears come. A couple of minutes later she had her cry and wiped her eyes.

"Silly woman thing to do."

"Good to see," Schoolboy said. "I haven't seen a woman cry since I left Chicago. Indian women just don't cry."

"I'll make up for it," Marleen said.

"Eventually, if the army makes you leave your land, which they almost surely will do in five, maybe ten years, Marleen and her ranch can rent it from you for grazing, and see that nobody else tries to take it over."

White Eagle nodded. "I was hoping something like that might happen. Now will you excuse me for a minute. My damn white training. I want to wash up."

He went to the bowl and washed his face and short hair and chest and back, dried carefully. Morgan had a clean shirt for him from his carpetbag when he was ready.

Morgan washed up next and they looked at Marleen. "Right now I'd guess it's time that you were taken out for a dinner you didn't have to cook."

Marleen fluttered. She was so surprised she cried again. Then she changed her dress and combed her hair until it shone, even when it was short around her head.

She held both their arms as they walked to the Nebraskan Hotel and into the dining room. They sat down at a table for four and a moment later the largest waiter in the dining room came up.

He looked at Schoolboy. "We don't serve Indians," he said softly.

Schoolboy stood quickly. "I beg your pardon, young man. Would you mind repeating that? I don't think I heard precisely what you said."

The waiter shrugged. "Boss told me to tell you that I can't serve you."

"If you would be so kind as to take me to this gentleman."

The waiter nodded and led the way to the front of the dining room. A small man with a full beard and a monocle seemed surprised when Schoolboy stopped and stared directly at him with a look of disdain.

"You're new here, aren't you?" Schoolboy snapped. "Your taste is abhorrent, your manners are disgusting, your monocle ridiculous and your morals not above reproach. You will serve me, and you will do so at once and with impeccable manners and courtesy. I don't want a waiter to do it, I want you. If you disagree with me, please call the hotel manager."

The manager of the dining room nearly fainted. He had not expected such a barrage from the Sioux. He had no idea who he was but the general rule was not to serve town Indians.

"I'll be glad to serve you, sir. Please let me take you back to your table. The dinner for your party is with the compliments of the house. May I suggest oysters on the half shell. They are fresh, only three days ago they were nestled deep in the Atlantic Ocean."

The dinner was delicious, and free, and they laughed all the way back to the cafe. Morgan insisted that Schoolboy take the bed. He rolled some blankets out on the floor and tried to get to rest. The throbbing pain in his shoulder kept him from falling asleep.

Sometime before midnight, Morgan sat up, left his blankets and climbed the stairs to Marleen's apartment over the cafe. She was sitting up waiting for him with a strained little smile that vanished when he came.

"You really meant it about wanting me to be your ranch manager?"

"Absolutely. You can make a lot more money than you will around here. After three or four years of building up a herd you should be able to clear twelve, fifteen thousand a year. Look at the money you'll save on a trail drive getting the critters to the rail line."

"You said you'll be around a while, six months or so to get started?" she asked.

"If it takes that long."

Marleen grinned. "I'm sure it will. For six months with you, I'll be happy to run your little ranch."

"Little? how big was your first ranch?"

"A homestead, a hundred and sixty acres."

They both laughed.

"Now, let's not talk about ranches," Morgan growled. "Let's talk about seeing how soft and tender and slow we can be making love."

They woke up after three A.M. and found new and interesting ways to delight each other.

"Six months?" Marleen said. "I won't know nearly enough about a ranch in six months. How about a year or a year and a half?"

"Who knows?" Morgan said. "It might be three

months, it might be a year. In this game we take things one day at a time, one problem at a time, and hope we know the answer and that we can stay alive."

"Shut up Morgan, you talk too much."

He showed her that he was an action man. They didn't get to sleep until a bantam rooster crowed at the first light of the new day.